Control Freak

DIARY OF A CARE LEAVER

Henrietta Bond

Published by
British Association for Adoption & Fostering
(BAAF)
Saffron House
6–10 Kirby Street
London EC1N 8TS
www.baaf.org.uk

Charity registration 275689 (England and Wales) and SC039337 (Scotland)

Reprinted 2012

British Library Cataloguing in Publication Data
A catalogue record for this book is available from the British Library

ISBN 978 1 907585 04 3

Project management by Miranda Davies, BAAF
Designed by Helen Joubert Design
Cover photographs by Lucia Reed
Typeset by Fravashi Aga
Printed in Great Britain by TJ International Ltd.
Trade distribution by Turnaround Publisher Services, Unit 3,
Olympia Trading Estate, Coburg Road, London N22 6TZ

BAAF is the leading UK-wide membership organisation for all those concerned
with adoption, fostering and child care issues.

Acknowledgements

There are so many people I want to thank for their help with this book that it's hard to know where to start. First, I have to mention the wonderful people at BAAF who have all been so encouraging and patient with me: Shaila, Miranda, Michelle, Jo and Ruth, I really am extremely grateful to you for turning my idea into something I can hold in my hand. Thank you, too, to Jake Coward, Lauren Harvey and Michelle Wright – all young readers who cast their critical eye over the early draft – and to Leigh Chambers for her constructive comments.

There are many young people over the years whose views and stories have shaped this novel, and organisations that work to give these young people a voice, in particular: A National Voice, Voices from Care (Cymru) and The Who Cares? Trust. Others whose insights into the world of care leavers have been invaluable include Ena Fry, Benni-Jo Tyler, Maxine McDermott, Simon Nixon and Tommy Turner. Research from the Care Leavers' Association has also been very helpful.

I want to thank my amazing husband Frank for his patience and understanding when I put the book before everything else. I'm also extremely grateful for the support and encouragement of Hilary Rock, Ian Peacock, Wilhelm Finger, Sarah Wragg, Sarah Algar and all my friends at Warren House; and Lesley Turner, a highly successful author friend, who is always so modest about her own achievements.

Finally, I have to mention someone whose robust attitude to life and commitment to justice has always inspired me. Patti Smith – poet, author, artist and singer/songwriter extraordinaire – your music is often the backdrop to my writing.

About the author

Henrietta Bond lives in Essex with her husband, three cats and a horse called Dingbat (who she swopped for a pound and a bottle of red wine). She's been trying to write a novel since she was nine, and first embarked on 'The adventures of Daisy, the disgruntled cow'.

To earn a living, Henrietta works as a freelance journalist and media consultant specialising in children and family issues. A former press officer for BAAF, since becoming freelance she has worked with Barnardo's, Fostering Network, The Who Cares? Trust, A National Voice, and many other children and young people's organisations, and local authorities. She has also written for *The Guardian*, *Community Care*, *Care and Health* and *Children Now* as well as authoring several BAAF books. This is her first published novel.

Note

Control Freak is a work of fiction. The book's characters are the product of the author's imagination and any resemblance to real people, living or dead, is purely coincidental.

Dedicated to the memory of Carmel Perry

THURSDAY 16 JULY
Day one of my new life

'You're not leaving! You can't leave us Holly! What will I do without you?' Lucy's my foster sister and my best friend, but if she says that one more time I'm going to throttle her.

She knows it's always been my plan to have my own place when I go to college. But Lucy says that just because you make a plan when you're 14 doesn't mean you have to stick with it when you're 17. I said that sticking to plans is important. Well, it is to me anyway.

'Is your plan more important than me? More important than Mum and Dad?' Lucy then asks. And I tell her that's a silly thing to say.

It's not that I don't like Jane and Martin – or their house. It's just that I'm more than ready for my own place. I've lived in other people's houses on and off since I was eight, when my mum started hearing the voices. Before I came here I lived in ten different houses – although one of them was a bungalow and one of them was a "respite place" so I don't know if those two count.

Lucy's parents, Jane and Martin, have fostered me since I was 12 when social services decided that my brother and I were never going back to our own home. Because they knew then that Mum was never going to make a proper recovery. And living here is the nearest thing to a family life I'm ever likely to get. So, of course they are very important to me. But that doesn't mean I want to stay in this house forever.

Because when I have my own home it's going to be perfect. Maybe not big or posh or anything very special to look at from the outside, but it will be my place and everything will be just how I want it. Which means I'll be able to find things coz they're exactly where I left them. Nobody will move my stuff or mess it up, or decide that maybe it's OK for them to borrow it, wear it or take it to school because they can't find their own iPod, jumper or gym kit.

Jane and Martin are good people. They've done well by me and the other kids who have lived in this house. Most of the kids come for a short time and then go again. Sometimes they're little kids and they're cute, and Lucy lets them come and play in our bedroom because she's got a thing about little children. But some of the older ones, the ones with too much attitude, they really get on my nerves. They think they're so smart and they give Jane and Martin a hard time. They're the ones who sometimes nick money from Jane's bag or take things like my CDs and makeup or things the other kids leave lying around. I don't really leave my stuff lying around. I leave it where it's meant to be – in the wardrobe, in the drawers, on the pegs or under my bed. But these kids still go in there when Lucy and I are out and they mess it up or take it for themselves. (They don't go to school because they're suspended or expelled or waiting for a referral into a special unit for difficult kids.) I told Jane she should put a lock on our door, but she just said that people don't put locks on rooms in their own houses.

We had a girl here last month who took stuff all the time. She'd take anyone's clothes out of the laundry basket and just wear them like they were hers. I'd see her going out in my new *Punky Fish* top and I'd ask her if it was hers. (I knew it wasn't but I thought I'd better give her a chance.) She'd say 'no', like it was the right answer, and that she found it in the ironed stuff and thought it was 'cool'. She wasn't guilty at all. But Martin said that she couldn't always understand things because she had some sort of learning disability, or whatever the PC word is for that these days. (You get to know all the right words when you've been in the system as long as I have.) Personally, I thought she was putting it on because that girl was dead good at maths. She was only 12 and she could do maths stuff I could hardly do for my GCSE. And when you took her shopping she added everything up in her head – so she knew what the bill was going to be before you ever got to the checkout. But she also did weird things – like the day she bit a man in the supermarket.

The girl was only with us another fortnight. Then she went back to her mum. She was crying the night before and I don't think she wanted to go. I don't think Jane or Martin were that happy about her going, but they don't have any say in these things. All the foster kids belong to the local authority so they can move anyone whenever they want. It's only when foster parents get a residence order – like the one Jane and Martin have for me – that you can even pretend you're part of the family.

These first pages of my "moving on diary" were meant to be about me and my new place but like always it's turned into a bit of a rant about those other kids. It's not that I really hate them or anything, but I get sick of them being around. I guess Lucy gets even sicker. After all, this is her parents, her house, her life. I don't know if anyone ever asked her if she wanted to share her bedroom with me. She was ten at the time and she probably thought it would be a good laugh having another girl to share with. Her brothers were gone to uni by then and she was the only kid left in the house. It's lucky really that Lucy and I get on so well. We've never fallen out – apart from a few small squabbles when we were younger. Having Lucy around helps me stop missing my brother Ryan so much.

Lucy drives me crazy with her untidiness and she's the most disorganised person in the world, but you can't help yourself from liking Lucy. Even when you're dead irritated with her. Everybody likes her, coz she likes everybody and she's always sweet and smiley. And nothing seems to worry her. Jane is always nagging her to do stuff – to get her homework done or tidy her stuff away – but Lucy never does it. 'That girl has her head in the clouds,' Jane said the other day, and I think she's right. If I was Jane I'd be tougher on my own daughter. Jane's always teaching some new kid to read, or hassling the education authority to give them a school place, and she's right behind me and my plans to go to college. But she never seems to bother much with Lucy – apart from nagging at her every now and again. Maybe she feels that Lucy ought to be OK coz she's had the privileges that the rest of us haven't. But I think it's hard on Lucy sometimes. I think Jane ought to spend a bit more time with her.

There I go again, getting off the point, and not writing about my moving on plans. Which is what this is all about. I started this diary as a kind of record – of me and how I moved out of care and into my own place.

Jane and Martin don't really want me to move out any more than Lucy does. They say I can stay with them while I'm at college coz there's a good one here in Corrington. But they do respect my decision – they've told me that. Because everyone knows I'm very organised and good at planning and doing what I say I'm going to do. And I've been saving like forever for this. Even my current social worker, Ahmina, who never manages to do anything without changing her mind a million times, told the people in the housing department that I wasn't someone they could mess around with.

And Jane's been brilliant and helped with lots of the forms and paperwork.

I should hear tomorrow which of the two flats I'm getting. I saw four last week but only two of them were any good. I want the balcony flat coz the rooms are larger and it's got a great view of the city. Ahmina says I should stand a reasonable chance of getting it coz they don't give balcony flats to young parents coz of the danger of the kids falling. I hope she's right. I really want that balcony flat.

Saturday 18 July
Day 3 of MNL

Yesterday disaster struck. Ahmina left a message on my phone while I was having a shower. She says that both of the flats I wanted have been given to other people. Apparently I don't count as a priority coz I'm not homeless. The council knows that Jane and Martin won't kick me out, and I know that too. But sometimes I wish they would. I've waited so long for my own space and nobody is going to take that away from me now.

I rang Ahmina back and told her that we should put in a complaint or something, but Ahmina said I just needed to be patient. I told her that my plan was to move into my flat at the start of the summer holidays – so I had plenty of time to decorate and get used to the place before college starts. I'd even written the dates on my year planner. But it's now two weeks since exams finished and no sign of me getting anything.

Ahmina said I wasn't the 'only fish in the sea' and that there were lots of young people in Corrington who were 'genuinely homeless'. Which I thought was a stupid thing to say. Kids in care don't have a family home to run back to when things go wrong so they deserve a proper place of their own – even if they're 17. I said

something a bit childish then, like 'It's not fair,' and Ahmina said
that life is very seldom fair. Which is probably true, but it made
me riled because Ahmina's husband is a barrister and they have
a large house up on Fairmount, where lots of the posh houses are.
So I then said something – which I knew would wind Ahmina up.
'I guess they've given my flat to some of those asylum seekers.'
And Ahmina said, 'Holly! I know you don't really mean that!'

I sort of wanted to say sorry to Ahmina because she was right
(one of the girls in my class was an asylum seeker and we signed
a petition to make sure she could stay here) but I hate losing face.
Because if you lose your dignity you've not got much left. So I just
said, 'Yeah maybe – but someone's got my balcony flat and it isn't
me.'

Ahmina tried to be kind to me then and went on and on about
how she was sure I'd get a place very soon. She promised to phone
up the housing people in the afternoon, after her team meeting.
'Can't you phone them before the meeting?' I asked her. And she
sighed and said she'd see what she could do. So I said 'thank you'
and tried to sound like I meant it. I know Ahmina thinks she's doing
her best but sometimes her best just isn't good enough.

I told Sean about it this evening, when we went out for pizza.
Sean is my sort-of-boyfriend. His dad has his own building
company and they have a really big house. Sean goes to the
grammar school on the other side of Corrington. He's doing four
A Levels because he wants to be a scientist or medical researcher
or something. He says he wants to be the first person to find a cure
for cancer, but I think it's coz he really likes cutting things up and
looking inside them. And his dad's friend's a nuclear scientist and
has this house in Mauritius.

Sean and I met at this school debating competition. We were
debating this topic, 'Democracy isn't everything it's cracked up
to be', and I was the second speaker in our team. I got to sum up

the argument and I said that democracy didn't do much for young people. If you don't have a vote and you don't get much say in decisions people make about you then it doesn't mean anything. I used an example of what happened to me when my brother and me were separated – and nobody was listening to me. Some kids don't like people knowing they are fostered but it doesn't bother me. I'm not ashamed coz I haven't done anything wrong. But Sean said I was brave to say that and he admired my openness. He wasn't speaking himself but was there to support one of his mates who was in the other team. He said he was glad my team won because we definitely made the best argument.

I thought that was a bit patronising but I could also see he really wanted to be nice. And I did fancy him a bit, so I let him take my number. He took me to an arty French film the first time we went out because he thought that's what I'd like – me being arty and all that. But I thought it was dead boring and so did he. But we didn't admit that till we'd been together for a few months.

Sean is kind and a bit quirky, and funny, and he can also be really deep. He keeps himself to himself, and he's into books and some really weird music stuff. He writes songs sometimes and he plays them to me with this guitar he got for his 13th birthday. He's got a nice enough voice but he says he's not very good. I tell him that if you think like that, then you never will be. Sean doesn't have that many friends coz he's more thoughtful than most of the guys his age. He's fit looking for a tall, thin bloke, but he's too thin for most of the girls round here, who want big meaty, brawny guys like the ones on *EastEnders*.

I've met Sean's mum a couple of times and she was nice enough to me, but underneath I could see she was thinking, 'That girl from care isn't good enough for my son.' What she doesn't realise is that I'm probably much too good for her son. I'll be the one who's a famous artist when her son is working in some lab testing things on white mice, or whatever it is they do in those places.

I'm not the sort of girl who always needs a boyfriend. Lucy is the loveliest person I know but she's always worried when she hasn't got a boyf. She says she needs to feel 'lovable' and know that someone thinks 'she's OK'. I don't get that at all. Maybe coz I have a lot more confidence than she does. If you only think you're OK because some boy fancies your legs, or your boobs or your hair, then that's just sad. You have to love yourself before you can expect anyone else to love you. And some people just won't be into what you have to offer. Which, quite frankly, is their loss – but that's the way life is.

Sean and I don't do couply stuff – like standing round the shopping centre and holding hands, while hanging out with mates. But it's nice to have someone to take me out places and stop other blokes hassling me. When you've got legs as long as mine, you can get a lot of unwanted attention. I don't go around in really short skirts or anything, but when I go out I want to look my best. And so many guys think you're putting it out there just for them. Some guys can be so arrogant, which is why I like Sean.

It's not that I don't fancy Sean; I mean he's a good kisser and I like that. But he isn't after just one thing, like all the other blokes around here. Not that he'd get it anyway. Everybody thinks girls from care are going to 'get into trouble' and end up as teenage single mums and all of that. I've got my whole life ahead of me, so I'm not taking any risks at the moment.

But Sean is good to talk to, by which I mean he's a good listener, especially when I have something on my mind. He doesn't tell me much about his own feelings but he's got lots of interesting ideas about politics and how the world works and he's always reading newspapers. So we're good at letting each other talk about the things that matter.

Sean believes in fate and karma and he thinks there just might be a god. He says he likes to keep his options open. He's quite a spiritual kind of guy, which is sort of cute. Before I met him I thought all that stuff was a load of crap but he's persuaded me. Just a little. Sometimes he makes me stop and look up at the stars. 'This does my head in,' he says, 'We can see the light of stars out there which are millions of light years away.' It's an awesome thought. It makes you feel quite little, like the small things you get hung up on don't matter that much. That helps sometimes because I'm the kind of person who tends to get narky when things don't work out.

Sean has this test. He says, 'Will it matter in a week's time? Will it matter in a month's time? Or a year's time? Or ten years' time?'

I tried to tell him that losing my balcony flat *would* matter in a year's time – and probably in ten years' time. I've put a lot of thought and effort into deciding what I want out of my life and I don't want some stupid housing person messing it up. If one thing changes, then everything changes – like that theory that a butterfly flapping its wings can change the future of the world.

In September, I start a BTEC in Art and Design at college and after that I'll probably have to do a one-year foundation course so I can apply to somewhere like St Martin's School of Art in London. I'm sure I'll get accepted there because my art teacher, Mrs Wilson, says I've got 'the kind of raw talent those places like'. While I'm studying I'm going to work really hard at my art, but I'll also get a couple of jobs, so I can save up for the future. I'm good at saving. I've been saving my EMA all year and when anyone says, 'What do you want for your birthday?' or something, I always ask for the money. That way I've already got quite a lot put away in my bank account. And I've always had a Saturday or holiday job or something. And my council's not bad at giving allowances for things. So I'm pretty flush as the moment. But you have to be prepared, coz when you get to 18 you don't get the same sort of support and you might have to manage on benefits. Some people who leave care get themselves into a right mess coz they don't know how to budget properly.

You just have to be careful and make the right choices. I know that I'm going to get a posh flat some day, and I'm not going to waste money now on loads of makeup or hair products or all that rubbishy stuff that girls at school spent their money on. Lucy's always buying some cutesy little dangly thing to go on her phone or some frilly new knickers or body glitter. I tell her she should be more careful but she doesn't listen to me. Which is stupid coz I've been managing money since I was a little kid and I did all the shopping for my mum and made sure the meter didn't run out or the electric wasn't cut off.

Often people tell me that I'm 'very confident'. I know what they really mean – which is that I'm far too sure of myself (Lucy calls me Miss Control Freak sometimes, but I hate that coz I'm not really like that). But I think self-belief is important. And planning. If you don't have a plan and lots of goals, then how are you going to achieve anything?

But Sean doesn't agree with me. He says that some of the best things in life 'just happen', which I think is daft. You could sit around forever waiting for things to happen and then bad things might happen to you rather than good ones. So you've got to have your own goals and work for them. I've always had to work hard at school. I missed a lot of education when I was moving around foster homes, but I wasn't having anyone think I was stupid. So I studied at weekends when lots of the kids at school were out wasting their time. But they're not ambitious like me; they don't want to be a famous artist.

Sean thinks I'm being silly about the flat. He told me that the balcony flat wasn't meant to happen. That if I'd have moved in there, the floor would have fallen through or something ridiculous. And that the right flat was still out there, waiting for me. I wish I could believe him but I know he's wrong about these things. You have to create karma by doing stuff – it doesn't just happen on its own. He thinks my idea of going into Ahmina's office on Monday is stupid. But it's not like I was actually doing anything important, just some football game down the park some of the kids from my old school have arranged – boys versus girls.

Sean was in an irritating mood tonight. He didn't take me seriously at all. I swear he was laughing at me when I tried to explain how everything depends on getting that flat coz I'll need somewhere to work on all my college art projects (just think what would happen if I tried to do that with all those kids around at Jane and Martin's!). Then when he walked me back to J & M's place and we stopped off in that bit under the trees for a goodnight kiss, he started getting a bit too passionate and his hands were going everywhere, and I wasn't in the mood for that. I pulled away from him and stormed off across the road. He tried to follow me but I ignored him, I slammed the door and went straight to my room. Jane heard me and came in to see what was wrong. Jane said I should tell him how I feel but then probably give him another chance 'because even sensible boys do stupid things sometimes'. And she also thinks there will be other flats.

Anyway, Sean texted me a few minutes ago to apologise for upsetting me and says he loves me and finds me 'irresistible', which is kind of sweet. I texted and said I forgave him. But I didn't say anything about love. I don't have time for love at the moment coz I have my whole life ahead of me. I think the only person in the world I really love is my brother Ryan – and that's because he's my brother. Sometimes he irritates me like crazy, especially at the moment when he hardly bothers to answer any of my emails or texts. I got a brief 'OK' reply when I asked if he was alright and the usual moan about his foster carers from him yesterday. But that's about the most he's managed all week.

Now I must get some beauty sleep or I won't be in the right mood to deal with Ahmina in the morning.

Lucy's just arrived home. I can hear her singing in the kitchen. I know she'll want to tell me all about her evening with the new boyf. She's just crazy about him. She lets him do *anything* with her, and I've told her she's stupid. But there's no telling Lucy. She thinks it's all OK as long as you're in love. What's it with all these people and being in love? You can't properly love someone you've only known for a few weeks, especially when you're not even 16 yet.

Maybe I can pretend I'm already asleep.

MONDAY 20 JULY
Day 5 of my new life

I'm really too tired to write this diary because I've been helping Jane with the new kid – this little boy who turned up at 10pm in a police car, with no clothes or anything of his own. Martin was out at his train society group. (Jane thinks it's just an excuse for all these men to get together and drink beer and play with train sets. Which it probably is, but who cares? Martin works in the Highways department of the council all week and then comes home and does homework with kids and sport and cycling and stuff all evening and each weekend, and takes them to swimming, and Brownies and dancing and judo. And sits in the police station when the older ones get themselves arrested. So I think he deserves a night off once a month to do daft stuff of his own.)

Anyway, Jane and I spent ages finding pyjamas to fit this kid and he looked at them like he'd never seen any before. And I made him spaghetti and toast because apparently he wouldn't eat anything else. And he didn't say anything, just kept chewing his nails – which were raw and bleeding round the edges. He stank bad when he came in but Jane gave him a bath and washed his hair, and talked to him in that special soothing way she always talks to new kids. I remember the first night I came here she talked to me like that – I wanted to hate her coz she wasn't my mum and I was furious with social services for making me go back to foster carers, but I couldn't hate Jane. She has that way of listening to you and talking to you – like she really knows how you feel – so you start liking her, despite yourself. She can be tough when she needs to, and she doesn't stand for kids messing her around, but Jane has a heart of gold. She's the best foster carer I've ever met. And I've met quite a few.

But I don't want to write about that now. I want to write about something that happened today. I don't know what to think about it yet and maybe getting my thoughts down on paper will help.

Ahmina was out of her office. Or so the receptionist said, but I told her I know they say that to everyone and as my leaving care worker, Ahmina has a duty to be there for me when I need her. But the stupid woman went on saying that Ahmina wasn't there. So I said I would just sit there until Ahmina came back. She said Ahmina wasn't coming back because she'd gone to a conference in London.

Typical, I thought: Ahmina's off on some jolly at the tax-payers expense. And I bet she hasn't rung the housing department. I guess some people would've left then, but that's not me – and I told the receptionist this. She just shrugged and said it made no difference to her. I was welcome to sit there all day – so long as I didn't wear the chair out.

That did it. 'Actually,' I said, 'I'd rather see Serena Allett – if she's still in the office. Or has the whole department gone to London?'

Serena Allett is the AD (which is assistant director) for children and families. I've met her several times. She came to the workshop Ahmina organised about being in care and she told me that I spoke very well. I think she'll remember me.

The receptionist (who I was starting to think of as Barbie's big sister coz her skirt was too short, her heels were too high and her hair was dyed that very blond colour that looks like it's made of nylon. And she had that wide-eyed plastic expression and cutsie-pie shaped mouth that looks kind of sweet on a doll but really dumb on a woman over 30) gave a big, bored sigh. 'She's out at the SWALK meeting today,' she said. (OK, it wasn't SWALK exactly but some other stupid word made up of meaningless initials.)

'OK,' I said, 'Just who is in, then?'

BBS just shrugged.

'Oh just ring the department and find out!' I snapped at her. 'Or shall I do it for you?'

'No need to be rude,' Barbie-woman snapped back. But she was wrong. I'd tried being polite and it was getting me nowhere. Anyway, she was prodding some numbers on the keyboard with her stupid long red nails and muttering something into the headset.

I flicked through my file. I always keep my own notes and bring them with me. Social workers keep files on you but they never seem to remember what's written in them, so it's best to keep your own. I have my Pathway Plan in front of me and I'm checking through it, when this tall black guy with dreads came in. 'Miss Richards?' he says, walking towards me and holding out his hand. He had one of those smiles that probably make some women go weak at the knees. And he had a pretty fit kind of body – which he was showing off in that denim shirt unbuttoned half way down his chest. But that sort of charm doesn't work on me.

'And you are?' I say, getting to my feet and holding out my hand. This sounded a bit ruder than I intended, so I gave him a small smile.

'Winston Jackson,' he says, grinning back at me like an idiot. 'I'm head of department – and Ahmina's boss. Let's go to my office.'

So I followed him to this titchy little office (if that's what the heads of department get, then it's clearly not a job worth having). But you have to give it to Winston – he was a good listener. He did a lot of nodding and saying 'uh-huh' while I explained the situation, and he didn't interrupt or scribble lots of notes.

I showed him my Pathway Plan. All kids in care are supposed to do a Pathway Plan when they're about 14 or 15. It's so you get a proper say in what's going to happen to you when you're old enough to leave care. It's got stuff like what exams you want to take, what course you want to do and the kind of jobs you want to get. And where you want to live. And it's all down in writing so the social workers can't pretend they don't know about these things.

Some kids don't seem to have much idea of what they want and they put stuff down because their leaving care worker or their teacher suggests it. Some kids put things in because their friends are doing it and they don't have any ideas of their own. My best friend when I wrote my Pathway Plan was a girl called Cat (short for Catriona). She was a bit older than me, funny, smart and she had this great way of dressing – really individual. She did amazing stuff with her hair and she really wanted to be a famous hairdresser. She lived with a foster carer who was good friends with Jane and Martin. Cat and I thought the same about lots of stuff, but I knew that messing around with people's hair was never going to be my thing, however much Cat tried to convince me that she'd have her own posh salon one day and her name on her own range of hair products. And sadly I was right – as always.

Cat went to live with her older sister in Ireland as soon as she was 16. She stopped answering my emails after a few months and her phone stopped working. Jane and Martin and the foster carer she'd lived with tried to find out where she was, but they were told that Cat's sister had moved away. Then about six months later, Jane came back from a training course, all red-eyed. She'd met an old social worker of Cat's who'd heard the news from someone else. Apparently Cat was in a car with some guy who'd been out boozing. The car went off the road on a corner and into a river. The rescue people couldn't get anyone out in time.

I'm glad I always knew what I wanted – which was to be an artist. But when I heard about Cat's death I did wonder for a bit whether I should try and be a hairdresser...like it could be some way to keep her memory alive. But I talked it over with Jane and she said that Cat would want me to follow my own dreams. I guess she was right and anyway, I think I'd be rubbish at cutting people's hair.

I'm writing about Cat and it's making me quite sad. But it's not really what I want to write about tonight. I'm getting off the point... which is that I showed Winston what was written in my plan – that after I'd done my GCSEs I would get my own flat, so I had somewhere of my own when I was at college. 'And just think,' I told him, 'You'd have another bed at Jane and Martin's for all those foster kids who you haven't got places for, if I moved out.'

That was a bit of a lie. Jane and Martin have said they probably won't take another long-term person like me, and Lucy's not prepared to share a bedroom with just anyone. Jane and Martin also say they'll always find a place for me somewhere if I need to go back to them. They say I'm part of the family like Lucy and her brothers. But that isn't really true. They've had money to look after me while I've been growing up and if I went back there when I'm older they'd probably have to keep me for free. And they shouldn't have to do this. It's not fair on them because it's not like I'm their blood daughter or anything.

'You're not exactly going to be kicked out. Some people stay on with foster carers until they're about 21 – or even 24 if they're still in further education. In this council our foster carers get paid for that. You do know that don't you?' Winston asked.

Did he think I was stupid? I've spoken at lots of conferences about the things that foster kids are entitled to. So I told him why I didn't want to do this. I've got to get used to being on my own and looking after myself – because there's no guarantee there's going to be anyone there for me when I'm older. And I need to have a home ready for my brother when he leaves care because boys are never as good at looking after themselves. So the sooner I start doing this the better.

I think Winston saw my point. But he told me that there's a real housing shortage in the area and while I'm not at immediate risk of being made homeless I probably shouldn't count on getting a flat straight away. He said that there are several other care leavers like me all waiting to get their own place. And two of them are pregnant so are much higher up on the list than me.

'So are you suggesting I get myself knocked up?' I asked him.

He smiled and said, 'You know that's not what I'm suggesting. I'm just trying to help you understand that while we totally support your desire to have your own flat, our hands are a bit tied at the moment. We have to fit in with the housing department and their priorities – we don't have a real say over how they allocate their flats. The only accommodation we have control over is our preparation for adult living houses – and I believe you've always said no to that option...'

He was rabbiting on and it was getting boring. 'Those halfway-house places are for kids who need a lot of support coz they aren't ready to live on their own,' I said.

Winston just smiled. OK, it was a nice kind of smile, but he wasn't half as charming as he thought he was.

'I don't need that kind of help,' I told him. 'I've always been able to look after myself. I looked after my mum and my little brother for almost two years before social services got involved. And Jane and Martin rely on me all the time – they say it's like having another adult in the house.'

'I'm sure they do,' Winston said. I knew he was sending me up a bit. I also suspected he was about to say something like, 'But all young people say that – they all think they are ready for independence but it's harder than you realise – financially if nothing else. Blah blah blah...' Ahmina says things like that sometimes and it makes me mad. I'm not 'all young people'. I'm me. I've got my own experiences and my own life.

But he didn't say that. Instead, he said, 'The level of support varies. If you don't need it then it's less work for the support staff. They can focus on the ones who do. And you do get a decent room to yourself – with a shared kitchen, bathroom and living room.'

I wasn't convinced but I had an idea. 'Could I live there – I mean, just till a proper flat comes up?' I asked. 'I'd still want my own flat, as soon as one comes up.'

'Sure,' Winston nodded at me. 'We don't often have vacancies in these places so we'd need your room back as soon as possible – for the kids who can't cope as well as you.' Now I knew he was mocking me.

'And if I say no?'

'Then you'd need to stay where you are for the moment – with your foster carers. Unless you particularly fancy sleeping on a park bench...'

'What about private rented accommodation?' I asked quickly. 'I know this girl who got her own bedsit in Fairmount...'

'Sure – but that wouldn't have been recently,' Winston says. 'Since the funding cuts, the committee decided that for under 18s we can only pay for supported bedsits, where you live in someone's house and they look out for you. I can't imagine you'd find that any more attractive.'

He was right. I don't need some kindly old lady popping in every five minutes to make sure I know how to switch on the kettle and don't burn my fingers on the cooker. I guess that would be good for lads who haven't been properly housetrained and some of the girls in my class at school wouldn't know how to open a can of baked beans without their mothers standing over them...

Winston is still talking. 'Anyways, there's one room going in St Mark's Crescent. Most of the young people living there are a bit older, students doing courses...'

I have a friend whose aunt lives in St Mark's Crescent. She works at the university, which is only a few roads away, and it's a fairly posh area. And a lot nearer to my college than Martin and Jane's house.

'OK,' I said. 'I might take a look at it. But I'm not committing myself to anything.'

'I'll get Ahmina to fix up a viewing,' Winston said.

'No,' I told him. 'That will take forever. Can't you fix something now?'

So Winston rang someone who rang someone else. I read a magazine and gazed out of Winston's window while this happened. And so I'm fixed up to go and look at the place at 4.30 tomorrow. Winston said that a worker called Phil could pick me up from Jane and Martin's, but I told him I'm quite capable of getting myself there on buses. So that's it – I will be going to have a look. I don't expect much but I suppose it's a start.

WEDNESDAY 22 JULY
Day 7 of MNL

If this was a day on one of those reality TV programmes, they'd probably say it was a good day because lots of things happened and people got angry or worried or upset. But that's not how I see it.

Ahmina left a message while I was having my shower. That Phil guy is off sick today and can't meet me. I phoned back and asked if she could meet me there instead but she said it wasn't possible, because she didn't have the keys. I said that someone was sure to let us in, but she said that wasn't the point. Phil worked there and he was the best person to show me round. It's no good reasoning with Ahmina when she's in one of those negative moods so I said, 'OK, tell him I'll be turning up tomorrow at 4.30, whether or not he's there.' Then I disconnected before Ahmina could say anything else. I hope she remembers to pass on the message.

I decided to go for a walk to calm down. I found myself walking near my old school and I decided to drop in. I thought Mrs Wilson might be around. She's the best teacher I've ever had and if it wasn't for her, I probably wouldn't be following a career in art. She believed I was good at art when the teachers at my previous schools didn't rate me at all.

I've been to quite a few schools since I was eight. You're supposed to stay at your own school if possible but sometimes they move you because the only foster carers they can find are too far away. Especially when they make an 'emergency placement', like they had to those times when my mum shut us in the house and threatened to set fire to all of us. Then you can end up in a strange school, and you don't know how long you're going to be there. So you don't know whether to try and make friends and get involved in things, or whether it's best to just treat each day as it comes.

When I was ten I went to a school where they were putting on an end-of-term play. I auditioned and got one of the best parts. I spent ages learning my lines and practised each night in front of the mirror. But then my social worker decided it was time for me to go home because my mum was out of hospital and wanted us back. Of course I wanted to go home, but I asked the social worker if I could stay – just another two weeks so I could be in the play. The social worker said there'd be other plays, and going home was surely more important than any play. I'd only been home three days when mum got taken back into hospital. And then we got moved somewhere else altogether, out in the country, where we stayed for about three months. And there was a different school that time. But I never got involved in any plays after that, I made sure I only did things that you could finish by the end of the lesson or the end of the week. That's when I started doing my paintings. If you have to, you can take them away with you and finish them – although some foster carers don't really like you using paint in their rooms.

When I started at this school, I'd been painting for a year or two but none of the other schools ever gave me much encouragement. At one of them this teacher called Mr Hutton tried to tell me that I should pay more attention to detail, learn to draw things accurately and not use so many bright colours. But Mrs Wilson was never like that. She said I had a 'great eye for colour', that I was 'creative and bold'. She never told me I had to tone down my colours or worry about whether other people saw things the same way that I did. She told me that great artists had their own way of seeing things and it was important that I developed my own style. And she also got me interested in learning about other artists. She lent me books and suggested exhibitions I might like to see. It was because of Mrs Wilson that I went to London for the first time. I got Sean to come with me and we went down by train to see the Tate Modern, which is this very cool gallery with a huge space in the middle and you go in down a ramp. It's a bit like going into a massive warehouse. Then the galleries are on floors round the edges and there's painting and sculpture and some exhibitions that are made from film or light and sound.

I want to make something like that one day. I like the idea of making paintings people could dance to. So people decide whether it's a fast track or a slow track, whether it's R&B or Indie or New Wave, or whatever they think the painting represents. I know it sounds a bit crazy but Sean understands what I'm talking about. He's writing a song at the moment about the colour of sound and how some days everything is pastel and soft lines but other days it's all primary colours and strong lines and angles. He says he got the idea when he was watching me paint and he was listening to this Muse CD. It was one of their albums from back in the day, not the recent stuff which he thinks is a bit over the top, with all that stadium rock stuff going on. He says that if he ever gets to perform any of his songs he wants it to be somewhere intimate, like the Cavern Club in Liverpool, where the Beatles and lots of those famous old bands got started.

I asked at the school office if Mrs Wilson was in but they said she wasn't, which is weird coz everyone's normally around in the last few days of term. I asked the secretary if she was ill or something, but she wouldn't tell me anything. She pretended like she didn't even know who I was although I only left a couple of weeks ago.

But Mr Leighton still remembered me. He's the deputy head, and he's a nice enough person but he's always in a hurry so he never gets to talk to anyone for more than two minutes at a time. All he ever says is 'hello' and 'how's it going?' but you find out soon enough that he can't stay around long enough to listen to an answer. Today he was saying goodbye to some official looking people with clipboards, when I approached him.

'Where's Mrs Wilson?' I asked him.

Mr Leighton looked anxious. Probably because he needed to be somewhere else and if he answered my question it would make him late. 'Mrs Wilson won't be in today – or again this term,' he said. 'She has family matters to deal with.'

Mr Leighton seemed to have forgotten that I'm not exactly a pupil any more. He was about to walk away when I stopped him. 'Please Mr Leighton,' I said, giving him my nicest smile, 'Can you tell me if she's OK? Is it her son again? Has he been taken into hospital?'

Once, when I'd stayed late to help Mrs Wilson put up an exhibition for parents' evening, she'd talked to me about her son. I could see she was upset and in the end I'd asked her if anything was the matter. She'd tried to tell me everything was OK but then she'd said she couldn't lie to me. She told me he'd been diagnosed with a brain tumour about a year ago, but then it seemed that he was starting to get better and it wasn't as serious as everyone thought. But recently he'd not been very well again. Sometimes after that she'd tell me little bits of news about him. Like when he was having some more tests or something.

I think Mr Leighton was surprised I knew so much. It made him realise I was quite close to Mrs W. He shook his head. 'No, not her son. Her husband had a heart attack last night. And he didn't make it.'

I took the bus into the centre and bought a card for Mrs W. I didn't want to get her one of those traditional cards with orange roses and gold lettering messages about "your sad loss". Instead I found a card with a photograph I thought she would like, just a simple black and white photo of a field on a hillside with a small tractor ploughing, followed by a flock of birds. There were bare trees around and the sky looked like it was about to rain. It had a sad feel to it, but it was also quite beautiful in its own way.

Martin was home when I arrived. He'd come home early because Jane has a training day (she's teaching foster carers to get NVQs in caring) and he needs to be around to look after the new kid, who doesn't seem to have a school to go to. The kid was at the kitchen table, doing something with pastry and Martin was doing something with jam – and I think it was supposed to be baking, but the kid looked all teary and Martin had that wrinkled look on his face that means he's been listening to someone really, really hard. I talked to Martin a lot when I first got here. Martin is probably the kindest person you could ever find, and sometimes just being listened to by him is enough to make you cry.

'We're making jam tarts but we're not sure if we've put salt or sugar in the mixture,' Martin tells me, hastily. He doesn't want the kid to be embarrassed by me seeing him upset. 'I think that Tobias was up to his tricks again before he left. We found flour in the sugar tin so we think the sugar may be in the salt tin. And the salt's in the sugar bowl. Or something like that. D'you want a cup of tea?'

Martin always makes me tea when there's something wrong. And I can see it in his face, there's something he needs to tell me. I need to make it easy for him, otherwise he'll tie himself in knots trying to break it to me gently. While all the time I'll just get more worried and frustrated with the time it takes him to break the news.

'What's happened?' I ask, pinning him with my best look.

'Ah,' he says, 'Clever Holly. You're always a mindreader.'

Silly man, I think. But he's also a dear silly man. Everyone loves Martin – even the really angry kids who think they hate everyone. It's lucky that Jane is as strong as she is. Martin is a softy through and through. Jane makes all the tough decisions for both of them, and she doesn't mind when kids hate her and curse her and give her a hard time.

'So what is it this time?' I ask Martin, but I have a pretty good idea. It's usually something to do with my brother, Ryan.

Martin nods towards the hall and we leave the new kid pounding his sadness into the pastry with a rolling pin. 'Donald rang,' he says, handing me a piece of paper with a scribbled phone number. 'He wants you to call him back asap. I'm around this evening so I can run you up to the station if you need to...'

Donald is Ryan's social worker. I don't need the number because I've got it saved on my phone. I've been talking to him a lot over the past two years. He needs to take a firmer approach with Ryan, but his heart's definitely in the right place.

'Hello Holly,' he says, recognising my voice. 'How are things with you? Got that college place sorted out?' He always sounds pleased to hear from me. I bet he wishes the kids he works with were half as together as me.

'Yeah, it's fine,' I tell him. 'So what's my brother been up to this time?'

It seems that Ryan has gone missing again, but this time it's been more than just one night. Ryan is pretty good at disappearing. Recently he's been doing it about once a month. He doesn't turn up after school at his foster carers and they start hunting all the usual places. Sometimes they find him by bedtime and sometimes before midnight. Sometimes he's picked up by the police and sometimes he just turns up for breakfast, and refuses to say anything.

'It's been nearly two days,' a worried Donald tells me. 'Kitty and Craig are off their heads with worry and I have to admit that I'm pretty concerned myself.'

It's hard to imagine Kitty and Craig off their heads about anything. Personally, I think they're part of the problem. They're not the right foster carers for Ryan and he knows it. Ryan thinks they don't care about him that much – not like Jane and Martin care about me. I've stayed with Kitty and Craig a couple of times and they strike me as the sort of people who think they are right about everything, and can't bear it when other people don't think they are perfect all the time. I think that's the real problem with Ryan. He comes across as a bit of a joker who doesn't care much about anything. He seems very easy going and laid back, but inside he's pretty sensitive. I don't think Kitty and Craig get him at all, and they nag him for stuff they should leave well alone. Ryan did OK when there was just me looking after him, but since we got split up he's become very stubborn. Some battles you can't win with Ryan and it's best not to go there with him. But Kitty and Craig just keep on and on at him. If Ryan says he won't do his homework, then I think they should leave him. Let him get into trouble at school – it's the only way he's going to learn. And if he doesn't, then there's nothing much you can do. You just have to let Ryan be. He'll sort himself out when he's ready. My dad was like that and maybe if my mum hadn't gone on at him so much, he wouldn't have walked out on us so many times.

These days my dad lives in America. The last time he and Mum split up he retrained and got this amazing job with computers. And he met this American woman, divorced Mum and got a transfer to New York. He still sends cards and letters and presents at

Christmas, and sometimes at birthdays, but he doesn't call or email or do anything other people's dads do. He writes that he'll come and visit sometime but he hasn't yet. I know he's got another child with this woman and it feels like he's almost forgotten about us. Ryan says sometimes he's going to run away and find him – it's no big secret where he lives, there's a P.O. address on all his letters so you could track him down if you could get to the right post office and make some enquiries.

Maybe that's where Ryan's gone this time, but I don't think so. He doesn't have a passport or any money, and I can't see him being organised enough to stow away on a ship across the Atlantic. I asked Ryan once where he goes when he runs away and he said 'random places'. I asked him if he went to mates or on his own and he said, 'Depends...' I know the police often pick him up sitting in some windswept shelter on the seafront. Ryan loves the sea and any place that's by the sea. His foster carers live about 40 miles from the nearest beach and Ryan hitchhikes or takes the bus. And usually once he's there he makes no effort to hide. They find him sitting somewhere really obvious, like the pier or a café, or in a deserted bumper car. But he's been gone for two nights now and the police haven't found him in any of the normal places.

Donald believes me when I tell him that I've had no messages from Ryan, but he asks me to let him know if I do hear anything. I say that I will and I guess I'll definitely do that, unless Ryan gives me a really good reason not to. I'm as freaked as anyone else by the idea of my 13-year-old brother roaming around the countryside on his own. After I disconnect from Donald, I try and phone Ryan but there's no reply. I send a few texts but I have this feeling that his phone isn't working. I even email and Facebook him – just in case.

The rest of the day was just a day. I wasn't much in the mood for anything after all that bad stuff. Sean texted to see if I wanted to go to some party a mate of his was invited to, but I said I wasn't feeling like it. He guessed there was something wrong and asked if I wanted to talk, but I told him I didn't.

I'd already had a good talk with Martin by then. I helped him cook the supper for the other kids and he let me talk as much as I needed.

Martin says that in life some things just happen to people who don't deserve them. And you don't achieve anything by wondering why it happens or thinking how unfair it is. He says that if I was religious he'd probably suggest that I pray for Mrs W but he knows that's not my thing. But he says I can still hold Mrs W in my thoughts and that sending her the card is a good move. He says that at times like this it really helps people to know that other people are thinking about them. So I spent some time after tea writing out what I wanted to say to Mrs W in rough, and I showed it to Martin. He made a couple of suggestions and I then wrote it into the card. I've put a stamp on it. Tomorrow I will give it to Lucy to take into school and ask the office to write Mrs W's address on it.

Martin doesn't tell me not to worry about Ryan – he knows I can't help worrying. But he reminds me that Ryan is my brother and he's got my survivor instincts, so he's probably pretty good at looking after himself. I wish I could believe him, because I'm not sure that Ryan is as tough as me. Ryan is a bit of a clown, but he gets very down sometimes. I think it was more difficult for him growing up with a mum who was so weird sometimes. I knew Mum before the voices started but Ryan doesn't really remember those times, and he asks me sometimes whether he's going to be a bit crazy when he grows up. I tell him he's already crazy, but in a really good way – and that there's no reason he's going to have a mental illness like Mum. I also tell him that lots of people have mental illnesses and learn to live with them perfectly OK – and that there are drugs and counselling and other things to help you. And lots of people suffer depression or have some kind of breakdown and you'd never guess there was anything wrong with them. It doesn't make them dangerous or a freak or anything like that.

Mum is just one of the very unlucky ones; she got really ill and she had a bad reaction to some of the treatments they gave her. And she hasn't got better so far. One day maybe she'll be OK again, and she'll remember that Ryan and I are her children. But I don't really believe that's going to happen and neither does Ryan.

I watch some stupid film on TV with Jane after the younger kids have gone to bed. It's one of those American movies where you know that the girl will get her guy at the end, but there's a lot of misunderstanding and crying before it happens. Jane and I sit there bawling our eyes out when it seems that the guy has got engaged to someone else, and the girl is talking about leaving New York and taking a job on some expedition to the North Pole. But then of course, it turns out that the guy realises he's made the biggest mistake of his life and climbs up the scaffolding outside her office window just to prove how much he loves her, even though he's petrified of heights. And of course she takes him back and then has to try and rescue him from this ledge where he's got stuck. And then she gets stuck too. So they're snogging the faces off each other by the time the emergency helicopter arrives.

Sean texts to say he misses me and hopes I'm OK. He says again that he loves me. After the stupid film I nearly text back and say I love him too, but I know that's not fair. I do sort of love Sean, a bit like I love Lucy, but I don't think I'm actually in love with him. He's a really good friend and he's pretty fit and sometimes he's great to talk to, but he definitely isn't the love of my life.

I'm lying in bed this morning, writing this journal because I've had a bad night. I don't have anything much to do until I go to see this place this afternoon.

Lucy and the younger kids are at school, and Martin's gone to work and Jane's out somewhere. Probably, knowing Jane, she's down the education offices giving someone a hard time about getting that new kid a school place for next term. So I've got the house to myself. It's just me and Boots, who is lying on my feet. Boots is an enormous black cat. We used to have his mum, Sasha, as well and Boots was one of her kittens. But Sasha died two years ago and now Boots is the only cat in the house. Boots is good at looking after himself. He knows which kids to avoid, and he can scratch if someone tries to tease him. I'm not really a "cat person" as my mum had this phobia about cats, but Boots is a cool sort of cat and I'm fond of him. I wish I could take Boots with me when I move. Maybe once I'm properly settled I could re-home a cat from the cat sanctuary. I wouldn't want a kitten because that wouldn't be fair. I wouldn't have enough time with my studies and my projects to housetrain a kitten.

Last night I went to bed before eleven and there was no sign of Lucy. I made a mental note to talk to Jane about this. Lucy is only 15 and she's still a kid in many ways. Jane would go loopy if one of us foster kids stayed out as late as Lucy does. But Jane thinks that Lucy needs her space – and I guess it hasn't been easy for Lucy growing up in a house full of kids that aren't related to her, who take up so much of her mum and dad's time. Jane seems to think that Lucy is very mature for her age and sensible – and that's probably because Lucy is always so kind and helpful to everyone. And her mum's come to rely on her for help with the younger kids. But Lucy's still a bit of a child really, she isn't tough underneath like Jane. If you opened Lucy up you'd find a big squishy marshmallow inside saying 'love me, love me'. But I hope no one is going to open Lucy up. I shouldn't even be thinking like that. I have to stop reading those vampire books that Sean lent me. They're not teaching me anything useful and they're not exactly improving my mind or expanding my horizons. Sean lent them to me because he said I should take a break from work after my exams finished, and read something just for fun. But I think Sean and I have different ideas of "fun".

Anyway, I fell asleep soon after I had those thoughts. But in the middle of the night – probably around 1am, Lucy came in and woke me up. She was definitely a bit drunk and she was giggling and being really stupid. I tried to ignore her but she sat down on the side of my bed and kept saying 'Hols, are you awake? I've got to tell you something!'

Lucy was dead excited because she'd "done it" again with her boyfriend. And this time he told her he loved her and had said something about getting engaged. I thought that was pathetic – they're both so young and they've only known each other a few months. My opinion is that he likes "doing it" with Lucy and wants to make sure she keeps "doing it" with him, so if he makes some random promises, she'll be happy to let him keep doing "it". But Lucy tells me she likes doing it as well and she can't get enough of him. I tell her that she'd better be using condoms as well as being on the pill, but she just laughs and says she 'wasn't born yesterday'.

Then Lucy tried to tell me what I'm missing out on, but I didn't want to listen. I'm not a prude or anything, just careful. I can wait till I find the right bloke and I'm not screwing my life up just for a quick grope in the dark. When I'm an artist with my own studio I will have time for lovers – and they will be clever and romantic and maybe look like that Pre-Raphaelite artist, Dante Gabriel Rossetti I saw on a TV programme. But he was really into himself and women fell at his feet. His poor wife even killed herself. But my men will work in films or TV or be successful writers, and they'll have money to buy me presents and take me out for posh meals and holidays. My men will have to wait their turn and I'll only see them when I feel like it. I couldn't imagine killing myself for the love of any man, that's so stupid. I don't think I'll ever marry anyone, though I quite like the idea of having some children. But not until I'm over 30. I have far too much to do with my life before then.

I wanted to tell Lucy about Ryan but I didn't think Lucy was in the right mood to listen. I told her to get to bed and she stumbled around a bit and then fell into bed in her knickers and bra. She lay on her back and started snoring. That's what too much alcohol does to you. It really gets on my nerves when people drink and act stupid. I want to shake them or kick them or something. Sean makes me mad when he drinks too much, I've walked out on him at parties a couple of times and he's now got the message.

Lucy's snoring kept me awake for hours. And then when I slept I had really bad dreams. I dreamt that Ryan had stowed away in the back of a truck going to America (although I don't think trucks really go to America, coz it's too far away). It was one of those refrigeration lorries that I saw a story about on the news. Some people from Eastern Europe had climbed on board and hidden inside – coz they thought they'd get a better life over here. But some of them were dead when they arrived in the UK and some of them lost their fingers and toes because of the cold. It was a stupid thing to do but I guess it shows how desperate some of those people are. I wish we didn't have to have all that passport and borders stuff and we'd just let people come and live here if they really want to. Who says this country belongs to us just because we happen to be born on this bit of land, and that we have a right to put up borders and say you can come here but you can't? We tell people it's good to want a better life for themselves but then we punish them if they try and come here to get it.

Anyway, Ryan had hidden in this refrigerator truck going to New York. Someone called me and said I'd better get to New York quickly. I went down the road and got on a plane (it was only a dream so it was OK for there to be an airport at the bottom of our road). The flight only took a short time, but all the way there I was worrying about what I was going to find. I was thinking about my brother and that daft smile he has. Where his mouth smiles and he raises his eyebrows at the same time, and you don't know if he's really smiling or sending you up. And he does these great impersonations of comedians from the TV – he knows some of their routines off by heart. And lately he's started adding things of his own. I think my brother will be a stand-up comedian when he's older, or an actor or something. But he says the kids at school say it's "gay" to do drama. I know it's difficult for boys of his age. There's lots of peer pressure and bullying, and boys are afraid of being different from everyone else, in case they get beaten up. But I'm getting off the point now. In my dream I kept wondering if Ryan was dead or alive.

I got off the plane in New York and I walked over some fields to the harbour. (It was only a small harbour but I guess whoever designs the sets for my dreams doesn't have much of a budget.) I could see the refrigerator lorry and lots of people standing around. Some bodies were being carried out on stretchers. I started hunting among the bodies, pulling back the blankets that were covering their faces, but under each blanket there was just a block of ice and you couldn't make out any features or anything. But I knew that none of those bodies was Ryan's. Then I went and asked some ambulance men who were putting stretchers into the ambulance. They let me into the ambulances to look at the people who were still alive, but my brother wasn't among them either. So I went back to the refrigerator van and a man was putting red tape across the doors. 'My brother's in there!' I shouted at him, but he just shook his head.

I was beating on the door with my hands and telling the people around me that they had to open the doors again and have another look. But everyone ignored me and started to walk away. So I started hunting around until I found a hammer, and I began smashing the door down with this. At first the door wouldn't shift but then it swung open. Inside the van I could see lots of weird shapes. They could have been giant icicles but I felt that something was wrong. I knew that inside one of them I would find Ryan. But each time I looked carefully at the icicle I realised there was nothing inside, just frozen water. The inside of the lorry seemed to go on forever and I was getting colder and colder the deeper in I went. I had this stupid thought that maybe if I went further inside it would turn into Narnia – but that's at the back of a wardrobe not a refrigerator lorry.

Then I saw something dark inside an icicle. It was kind of body-shaped but I couldn't be sure if it was a body or not. The more I tried to look, the more I couldn't decide what was inside it. So I started chipping away at the ice with my fingers but I couldn't seem to get through. I was getting colder and colder all the time.

I woke up to find that the duvet was on the floor. I'd left the window wide open because it was quite a hot night when I came to bed. But it's been a funny kind of summer and the temperature changes that quickly. So I went downstairs and made myself a mug of tea and ate some of the digestive biscuits with the caramel layer and chocolate on the top. And then, coz I was feeling warmer I had some caramel and toffee ice cream from the freezer. Usually it's the little kids who raid the kitchen at night. We even had one girl who used to eat everything she could find in the fridge – frozen peas and fish fingers and raw broccoli. Jane told me that this girl had been almost starved by her parents when she was little and she'd developed an eating disorder as a result. You'd never think it looking at the girl as she was so thin. But I often heard her being sick as I went past the bathroom, so I guess she'd become bulimic as well. I wanted to feel sorry for her but she wasn't a very nice person. She was always flying into rages and throwing stuff at people. Eventually she stuck a fork into one of the other kids and Jane and Martin decided it wasn't safe for her to stay here because of the younger children. Jane told me that social services found her a foster placement with a middle-aged woman who lived on her own and could give the girl the individual attention she needed. I hope she's doing OK there. Jane calls her sometimes and says she sounds a bit happier.

I was making a second cup of tea when the door opened. It almost made me spill the water from the kettle all over myself. That new kid stood in the doorway, just staring at me. He was probably pretty startled as well. I was trying to remember his name so I could say something reassuring to him. He had this hunted look in his eyes like he was waiting for something awful to happen at any minute. He started to back away, so I spoke to him.

'It's OK,' I said, 'It's OK to come into the kitchen at night. Jane and Martin don't mind, so long as you don't eat all the food or turn on the taps and leave them running, or play with the carving knives or anything...' I was rambling a bit because I wasn't really awake. And eating the ice cream had made me feel shivery and a bit strange.

The kid just stood there staring at me, like he'd seen a ghost. I think he's about seven but he could be older and just a bit small for his age. Jane and Martin probably told me when they announced that the boy was coming, but I don't always listen to all the details. So many kids come and go here that I don't have time to think about them all.

'D' you want a hot drink?' I asked the boy. 'We have hot chocolate or Horlicks. Or there's some cold banana milkshake stuff if you like that?'

The kid didn't say anything but he walked in and sat down at the table. I asked again what he wanted to drink and he nodded when I mentioned the banana shake stuff. He watched me carefully while I made it for him. If you just put it in the glass with the milk it sometimes goes lumpy, so we have a special shaker thing that Martin bought from Ebay. And we always have coloured straws for the drinks. Martin buys those as well. Sometimes he has milkshakes with the kids because he's just a big kid himself. I told the new boy all this while I made his drink. He watched me, hardly blinking, but he didn't say anything.

I gave the kid his milkshake and finished making my cup of tea. I sat down at the table with him and I offered him what was left of the packet of biscuits. He took one very carefully, watching me all the while. Then he nibbled it round the edges, like a little mouse nibbling at a piece of cheese.

The kid's silence spooked me a bit so I started talking. I told him that I had got up because I'd had a bad dream. I didn't go into details because it's not nice stuff to tell children, but I told him I

knew I'd had the dream because my brother has gone missing.
I also told the kid that I knew my brother would turn up safe in a
day or two, because he always does. I don't know why I said this,
but it's probably because I didn't want to frighten this nervy little
creature. He looks like he's scared of his own shadow. It's hard to
believe that he's been excluded from school for difficult behaviour,
but something I've learned is that kids who are mixed up behave
different ways in different places.

I asked if he had any brothers and sisters and he shook his
head, very quickly. But something in the boy's eyes told me he
was lying. But when you've been around kids from difficult homes
for as long as I have, you learn not to ask too many questions. I
hated it when people asked lots of questions about my own family,
so I respect other people's right to keep things private. Then I
noticed that the kid was crying. Big tears were pouring down his
face and splashing into the milkshake. He didn't make any effort
to wipe them away but just let them fall. I didn't know whether to
say anything so I just got up from the table to fetch some kitchen
towel. I pulled off a piece and handed it to the boy. He took it
from me and held it tightly. I watched him scrunch it into a ball
in his hand, as the tears went on streaming down his cheeks.
Then his shoulders began to shake and he started to sob. Big
sobs that sounded like his heart was breaking inside that skinny
chest. I moved my chair beside him and he leaned his head on my
shoulder, and went on sobbing and sobbing. I didn't say anything
much, just murmured stuff like 'It's OK, it's OK', which is the kind
of thing Martin and Jane say when a kid is really upset. If the boy
wants to talk he'll talk, but maybe all he needed to do was cry.

After about 20 minutes his crying stopped and he drank the
milkshake, very carefully down to the last drop. Then he got up
and left the kitchen, closing the door behind him.

I knew I wasn't going to sleep after that, so I went into the living room and put on the TV. There was a creepy looking film on and I wasn't in the mood for that, and something about fishing in Scotland. I found one of those educational programmes they show at night, which was trying to explain how easy it is to understand Quantum Physics. I think I must have dozed off during the bit about parallel universes because when I woke up the sun was streaming in through the windows and Martin was shutting the curtains to try and keep it from disturbing me. When he saw I was awake he offered to make me a cup of tea but I said no, I'd just go back to bed. Martin always gets up early. He does the kids' packed lunches and leaves everything ready for breakfast before he sets off to work.

Lucy was curled in ball, hugging that floppy giraffe she's had since she was little and sucking her thumb. She does that sometimes. It's kind of sweet, but I bet she'd be really embarrassed if she knew I saw it. I wish I had something of my own to hug but I got rid of all my kids' stuff when I was about 12. And I'm not a big fan of soft toys or cutesy things. Sean knows never to buy me those kind of presents. I'd rather have a CD or a book, or a new drawing pad. So I just hugged my pillow instead and I drifted off very quickly. Until it was gone nine o'clock and everyone was gone except me and Boots. And I dozed for a bit longer and then decided to write this diary. But it's time to get up now. I'm starting to feel like a slob, lying in my pyjamas and doing nothing. And there's still a smell of toast in the house and it's starting to make me hungry.

Later

This afternoon I went to see the flat. I arrived early – as I always do – and of course that Phil was late. He arrived all earnest and out of breath and very apologetic, muttering something about traffic and getting held up by an emergency phone call (if I had a pound for every time I've heard that excuse from a social worker

I'd be a multi-millionaire by now). Anyway he seemed nice enough but a bit disorganised. He spent ages emptying his pockets and looking for a key and started talking about running back to his car to see if he had dropped it, so I said let's ring the doorbell, and he looked sheepish and said he'd rather not. But I'd rung it by then so it was too late. 'It's OK,' I told him, 'when someone answers we can pretend I got here first and rung it before you came.' But he didn't seem very happy about that. I rang the bell again, as ringing once usually isn't enough. After a moment he said, 'Nobody's in,' and he ran off – presumably to look for his keys.

But someone was in. There was the sound of footsteps and then the door swung open. 'Hey man – give me a chan...'

But the voice stopped mid-sentence as the speaker saw me and realised his mistake. And my first thought was what incredible green eyes he had – because I really couldn't see much except this bloke's eyes shining in the shadows, coz he'd got this woolly hat thing pulled down over his shoulder-length brown hair.

'Ah,' he said, 'Saul's gone out but he's left me his keys. He can't get back in without them. And the buzzer's broken...' he trailed off, smiling now. 'But as I don't know who you are, you may be someone trying to sell me cheap electricity, or join me up to a cult, or persuade me to take out life insurance. Or maybe you're just a burglar come to check out the joint. In any case, do come in...I don't live here and I have no idea if I'm supposed to let you in or not.' He had this grand and rather silly way of talking, like he was a character out of a costume drama or something. But there was an edge of real humour in his voice and I quite liked listening to it.

'I'm Holly,' I said quickly, looking over my shoulder to see where Phil had got to. 'And a social worker called Phil will be coming back any minute now, to show me round this place. I think he's sort of in charge here or something...' I wanted to warn the guy with the green eyes in case he wasn't meant to be here. I know some of these places have very strict rules about guests.

'I'd probably better make myself scarce then,' Mr Green Eyes stepped away from the door. 'Just say someone buzzed and let you in. It was cool to meet you though Holly, however briefly. I'm Tol by the way, though that's not exactly my real name which is Ptolemy – after an Egyptian pharaoh or a Greek astronomer. You can take your pick.' And he turned round and bounded up the stairs, two or three at a time, leaving me standing at the bottom like an idiot.

At the top he called down to me, 'You spell that P-T-O-L-E-M-Y by the way. The P at the beginning is silent and the Y at the end gets pronounced like it's a long E. So it's kind of T-O-L-O-MEE. But most of my friends call me Tol. Just in case you ever need to know!' Like I ever would!

Phil appeared just after that, waving a set of keys. He frowned when he saw I was already in the hallway. 'No good getting into the front door, unless you also have the keys to the flats,' he told me. 'The one with the spare room is on the second floor. There are three flats here, with two people sharing each one.'

On the first floor there was just the hall and the staircase. And a door with a handpainted sign saying 'HQ'. 'Is that your office?' I asked Phil.

'Sort of. It's also a kind of flat if one of us is staying over.' Phil shrugged. 'I kind of share it with Cathy, the other house warden, and I also have desk space over in Cannonbury Road, and Cathy's currently working part-time at the Bay Trees Project. So we're here sometimes and there sometimes – and out and about most of the time. We're not around here keeping a check on you all the time, if that's what's worrying you. We used to have a duty worker sleeping over nights but we stopped that recently – due to the cuts. And it's probably better really. It's not helping anyone to be independent if they know we're hanging around all the time. But one of us always calls in around 8.30 in the morning to make sure everything's OK, and there's an emergency phone number you can ring if you need us at any time.'

Very reassuring, I thought. Just what you need: a friendly social worker barging in on you when you're trying to get ready for college, or recovering from a late night and wanting a bit of a lie-in.

I followed Phil up the stairs. 'This is Flat 1,' he said, indicating a door which clearly said 'Flat 1' in large letters. 'This is Keesha and Nathan – the flats are normally male or female, but those two are sister and brother, although he's younger than her. They're in sometimes during the day – I could introduce you.'

Today there's no one answering Phil's knock and after a moment he continues up the stairs. 'And this is Flat 2, where we have a spare room...I don't think Mel will be in at the moment coz she's usually at work at this time.' Phil knocks twice but when there's no answer he uses his keys. As he opens the door I have a strong sense that there's definitely someone in the flat. I just hope Mel isn't doing naked yoga or something in the middle of the living room.

Fortunately there's nobody in the living room – naked or clothed. Just a rather plain looking room with random furniture, empty bottles, greasy pizza boxes and overflowing ashtrays. 'Smoking isn't really allowed in these flats but as both Mel and the last girl, Sharon, smoked, we kind of turned a blind eye to it...'

'I can't live with smoke,' I tell Phil as the stale smell of nicotine worms its way into my nostrils and makes my eyes water. 'I couldn't live in here.'

Phil looks at me with surprise. I bet he's one of those social workers who thinks that all young people in care smoke – and do drugs.

'We could have it steam cleaned before you move in,' Phil says, heading towards a door. 'So this would be your bedroom. Sharon moved out about three months ago so it's probably looking a bit empty and shabby.'

But the room in front of me isn't empty at all. It's full of stuff, male stuff. And the owner of the stuff is lying on the bed. In football kit.

'What the...!' the lad sits up. He's broad shouldered, muscular and almost menacing as he glares at Phil from outraged eyes. Except he can't be more than about 16 and he's quite short for his age.

'Nathan! What the heck are you doing here?' Phil says. Then a look of uncertainty crosses his face. 'Have you guys swapped flats or something?'

The black boy on the bed raises his hands in a theatrical gesture and swings his feet to the floor. 'Man!!! Don't you and Cathy never speak to each other?' he demands, exasperated.

'I...no, sorry, we've both been pretty frantic recently. She probably sent me an email or something and...'

But the boy isn't listening. He's talking to Phil now, like he's speaking to a very small child. 'Me and Keesha fell out – which I told you about when you was last here. She won't have me in the flat no more coz she says she's sick of my sports stuff smellin' gross around the place. And Mel says she's lonely since Sharon's gone, so she move downstairs with Keesha. And I move up here – 'bout a week ago. Cathy said it was OK with her.'

'OK but...I mean this place is like a tip, there's food and fags all over the living room...'

'Not me – not the ciggies. It's Mel. That girl, she smoked like a chimney,' Nathan now looks like a rather annoyed puppy, as he points accusingly at the floorboards.

Phil's looking very flustered. 'I'm really sorry, there seems to be a bit of a mix-up,' he says to me.

But I'm starting to feel a bit better about this flat. Boys – especially boys as young as Nathan, who have football posters all over their walls – are definitely easier to manage than girls. Another girl can get really nasty if you move into her territory, but boys aren't like that. And boys don't usually mind if you start clearing things up, so long as you do most of the work. Besides, this boy looks young enough to be trained.

Also I'm beginning to hatch a plot which involves my own brother Ryan. If Nathan and Keesha can have a place together then surely me and Ryan can live together. Nathan looks a nice enough kid, but I'm sure if I put my mind to it, I can get him to return to living with his sister. Of course, that will mean getting rid of Mel, but if Mel's a heavy smoker then she shouldn't be in the building, because it's a health risk for everyone and could cause a fire.

'I've shared with boys all my life – we have lots of male kids at my foster carers. So long as there's a lock on my bedroom door, and the bathroom door has a lock, I won't mind at all,' I tell Phil as he ushers me into the hallway.

I insist on looking at the rest of the flat while Phil flaps around, urgently prodding at his Blackberry. I can hear him typing furiously as I inspect the state of the other living areas. Actually it's not too bad. Nathan has obviously made some effort to keep the bath and toilet clean and there's not that many unwashed plates and pans in the kitchen sink. And Mel's recently vacated room looks OK too. She's at least had the decency to give it a dust and vacuum.

'This will need to be fumigated and have a coat of fresh paint and a new mattress before I move in,' I tell Phil, who starts to trail around after me, his eyes darting nervously between his phone and what I'm doing. 'And the living room needs the same – the carpets and the cushions and seat covers need to be steam cleaned,' I say. 'If the council don't have their own cleaning people then my foster dad knows someone with their own cleaning firm.'

Phil goes onto the outside landing to make a call. And Nathan comes out of his bedroom to take a look at me. 'You going to be my new flatmate?' he asks. 'It's OK here. Nobody comes round botherin' you. Serious. Cathy an' Phil, they're not round much. An' when they here, they're most likely busy down in their office.'

'Who's in the upstairs flat?' I ask Nathan, remembering the guy who'd answered the door.

'This Steven – or Stephan. He got here like a month back...And this guy Saul. He's been here since before me and Keesh move here.'

'And Tol something? Is there someone here called T-o-lo-m-ee?, I ask, trying to remember the way the strange green-eyed boy had pronounced his name.

'A friend of Saul's or something...?'

Nathan shakes his head. 'Nope. No one here called that. But we don't see them much, them upstairs. They comes and goes when we're not around.'

That's a good thing really. There was something about that boy with the green eyes. It would be awful to start fancying someone I have to live with. It would make life much too complicated.

Phil saw me out. He said that so long as he could clear it with Cathy and his manager, I could share the flat with Nathan.

I tried to ring Ryan on my way home. He's still not answering, so I sent him a text telling him he has to call me.

Lucy has just come in – she's looking all red eyed and her hair's a mess. I'd better stop writing and talk to her.

THURSDAY 30 JULY
Day 15 of MNL

So much has been going on and I haven't had any time to write this diary. And I don't have much time now, so I'd better make this bit as short as I can.

Ryan was found on Sunday morning in a right state – and I went up on Monday to visit him in hospital. He'd got beaten up and his phone and money taken. He'd run away for a day but met some older kids with a van, who seemed OK at first. Ryan went with them but got scared when he found they were planning some sort of crime. He got away from them and slept rough in some seaside town, where he was set on by a local gang who took his phone. He tried to fight back but he's not exactly a big lad, and they really laid into him. He's got bruised ribs and cuts and scratches all over. He's lucky really that he's not hurt a lot worse.

My brother is really shaken up. Normally he can see the funny side, whatever happens. This time he seems so depressed. I read in this leaflet they gave us at school that boys can get depressed even more than girls coz boys often bottle up their feelings and don't talk to anybody. I told Donald that Ryan needs to live nearer me, so I can be there for him. Donald agrees. He also agrees that

Kitty and Craig aren't the ideal foster carers for Ryan but he says that getting placements for a lad of Ryan's age isn't easy. I told Donald about my new place and how there might be a space there for him, if someone moved out. Donald said it sounded good but Ryan would probably have to be over 16 before he could do that. I told Donald that I knew a girl of 18 who was made guardian of her little brothers and sisters so she could care for them; so maybe I could apply for that when I was 18. Donald said maybe.

Which brings me to Ahmina, who's probably less together than any other social worker I've ever had. At first I thought Ahmina was being snotty because she didn't like the fact that I'd fixed up the flat with her manager, while she wasn't around. But it turns out there's a problem with some paperwork that has to be sorted out with the finance people, and Ahmina'd got herself into a bit of a flap about it. But then Martin said he'd talk to her, because he's good at finance stuff and might be able to help. She came round here and I left her and Martin sitting round the table drinking mint tea and eating chocolate fingers, with heaps of forms all around them. I couldn't stay because Jane needed to run me to the train. Jane offered to drive me up to Kitty and Craig's but I said that the younger kids needed her and it would be good experience for me to travel on my own.

Hopefully, I should be able to move in next week. I've given Phil the number of the man with the cleaning firm and he's promised to get it sorted before then. I must ring him tomorrow to check that he's done it.

Jane and Martin still don't really understand why I'm moving to the room in St Mark's Crescent. They say I don't need preparing for adult living coz they can do that for me. (Not that I really need much preparation anyway.) I've tried to tell them that I don't want to be a burden to them any longer, but they don't seem to want to hear that. They say I'm part of the family and I should stay as long as I want to. They're not kicking Lucy out and as far as they're concerned I'm the same as Lucy.

But I'm not the same as Lucy – because she's their blood daughter. They've never been paid to look after her, so that makes it a different thing altogether.

And Lucy is also the third thing on my list. At the moment she's got herself in a right mess. And it's hard to help her. One day it's on with Daniel and he's all over her, and the next day he says he doesn't want to see her. She goes out with him and comes in all loved up and happy, then he texts her – at midnight or the next morning – and dumps her. So she cries all day. Till he texts that evening and says he's changed his mind and when can he see her.

I tried to talk to Jane about it the other night, but she said that being 15 isn't easy – especially when you've got a heart as tender as Lucy. And that not all young people are as together as I am. But I think something isn't right here. I asked Lucy the other night if Daniel hit her or anything like that, but she got all defensive and said no, he definitely didn't do that.

And there's another thing. Something that neither Lucy nor I want to think about, but I know it's worrying her a lot. Lucy's late this month and she's trying to tell me that her periods are always late, but that's not true. Sharing a room, Lucy and I have got into a bit of a pattern. We always come on at the same time. 'It's just my body complaining coz you're leaving me,' Lucy told me, in between crying about the dreadful Daniel. 'I wish you wouldn't go. I wish you'd stay. I'll miss you so much Holly.'

Lucy has always known I was going when I finished school. I've told her my plans hundreds of times, but Lucy has this way of not thinking about things till they happen. 'You can come and stay with me – I won't be far away and we can meet up most days, or you can stay over for the night. I'm gonna get a sofa-bed with the money I saved from that Christmas job,' I tell her.

But now I have to do a big sort-out and start my packing. I also have the shopping list I put together after I read this book about leaving care that Ahmina gave me. It gave lists of all the things you need when you get your own place. I won't need most of them for this place coz it's already got furniture and cups and plates and a TV and a washing machine. I've got my laptop which social services bought me and I've checked out that St Mark's Crescent has an internet connection. But I want to get some matching bed linen and towels. Jane's given me some stuff from the cupboard here, but most of it's a bit old. I don't want to seem ungrateful but I want some new things for my room, because it's the first time in many years I've had a room all of my own. And anyway, if I get some decent ones in a sale or something and look after them properly, then they'll last forever. Maybe in a few months I'll have a flat of my own but for the moment I'll have to settle for just a bedroom to myself.

Ahmina says I'm entitled to a small grant to help me buy essential stuff for my place but I've always saved my money till I really need it. So I'll probably invest the grant money in a building society or something, so I can make a bit of a profit and then I'll be able to buy big items of furniture when I get my real place.

Sean is taking me out for dinner tonight because it's his 18th birthday. There's a very posh new restaurant in town and his dad has given him the money to take me there. His dad is also lending him his car. I wish Sean had a car of his own; I really should have a boyfriend who has a car.

Later

The restaurant was nice but Sean spoilt it by wanting a heavy conversation. He started saying that he never knows where he stands with me, and how he'd like us to move on to the "next stage" of our relationship. It's great the way boys can find such fancy words for such basic things. I knew exactly what he meant but I pretended I didn't. On the way home he suggested that we went back to his house for coffee, because his parents were staying over with friends for the night. I told him that I needed to be home because I had a lot to do in the morning. (I want to go round to the flat and check some measurements. I've decided I'm going to make myself some curtains as the ones already there are bound to stink of nicotine. And anyway, the pattern was really naff. There's this really cheap market stall and the man there sometimes lets me have cut-offs and bits and pieces free or at a big discount, coz I went to school with his daughter. If I sew some of the bits together I think it will look good, kind of alternative. Like the sort of curtains an artist ought to have.)

Sean went very quiet at this point and he wouldn't talk to me for the rest of the journey home. I thought maybe he was annoyed that he'd only had Diet Coke all night while I'd had a couple of glasses of wine. But when I asked him what the matter was he said that I 'already knew'. I told him that if he thought I'd be ready to jump into bed with him because he bought me (or to be honest, his dad bought me) a fancy dinner, then he was a sad, sick person. He said that I was the sad one. He'd been thinking for ages about how nice it would be to spend an evening together – we could cuddle up and watch a late-night movie, there was even some sparkling wine in the fridge. And if something happened then it happened, but he wanted more than anything just to sleep with me in his arms. He said he wanted to lie with his head buried in my hair and to wake up and see me sleeping beside him. We could sleep on the sofa in our clothes if that was what I wanted. He just wanted to be with me, because he loved me.

I told him this was emotional blackmail. And he swore softly under his breath. When he pulled the car into Jane and Martin's drive I went to kiss Sean goodnight and he moved away. But I felt something wet fall onto my cheek and realised that he was crying. I tried to say something to him but he told me just to get out of the car. I said we would talk in the morning and he said 'maybe'. And he drove off almost before I'd closed the car door.

I can't sleep now so I'm watching a movie on my own in the living room, and eating chocolate ice cream with some of that swirly cream that comes out of a can. I didn't have anything from the dessert trolley in the restaurant because I was full up at the time, but now I really fancy something sweet. I texted Sean a couple of times to thank him for the evening and to say I was sorry we fell out. But he hasn't replied. Boys are so immature sometimes. I think maybe it's time I dumped him. I can't really see how he's going to fit into my new life and I'm bound to make loads of friends at college.

MONDAY 3 AUGUST
(no longer sure which day it is, so going to stop this system and count from the day I move to my new place)

It's been crazy again. And I still haven't organised half the things I need for my move.

They arranged another visit for me to go and see Ryan. He was out of hospital and back with his foster carers but they said he was really down, and they thought I might be able to cheer him up.

Donald picked me up from the train on Friday afternoon, to drive me to Kitty and Craig's house. We had a long chat on the way because Donald is really worried about Ryan, who is getting more and more withdrawn. He said that Ryan won't talk to anyone and maybe I can persuade him to talk to me – because nobody could work out what's going on with him. I said that it's simply that Ryan doesn't like his foster carers that much. They're not mean to him or anything and I think they do try to be nice to him, but he's never felt properly at home there. You can't be happy somewhere where you don't feel that you fit in.

I asked Donald whether it wouldn't be best to move Ryan into one of those group homes for a while. I was in one myself once, and they're not a bit like those old-fashioned children's homes they have in that film about Oliver Twist. You don't get fed gruel and you don't get beaten or sleep in dormitories with rats running around. There's only about 10 or 12 kids, who all have their own bedrooms or share a room with just one other person. And there's a TV and living rooms and OK staff, who look after you quite well. And you get to choose the food and do some of the cooking at weekends, and there's sports and outings and little parties for people's birthdays. And instead of rats there's tropical fish or a guinea pig or something.

But Donald said that in his area all the "residential units" have been closed down and all kids get placed with foster carers. He said that only "very troubled children" go to special houses in the community where there's one kid and about ten staff to get them ready to move on to fostering or, if they're still young enough, to be adopted. Ryan isn't really difficult or aggressive or anything like that, so he wouldn't qualify.

I asked Donald about finding other foster carers for Ryan but he said he'd already thought about this and can't think of anyone at the moment. Lots of foster carers are happy to take babies and young children – sometimes big groups of brothers and sisters – but not everyone will take teenage boys. Kitty and Craig are the best carers for Ryan at the moment till the council recruits some new foster carers. I asked how long this is going to take coz I know new foster carers don't grow on trees. And of course, Donald couldn't give me a proper answer. (Every year there are campaigns on the TV asking people to think about fostering, but Jane says that many of the people who come forward haven't a clue what they're letting themselves in for. They want cute newborns or kids without problems and they run a mile when someone tells them that lots of these kids have been messed up in some way – neglected or abused or interfered with. Or they might be very disabled, or not quite right in the head or do poos and smear them all over your walls. And the ones who don't get put off by that are put off by the thought of having to meet the kids' mums and dads. Jane always laughs about this – she says that it's far more frightening for the mums and dads to come and visit their kids in someone else's house, coz they probably feel everyone is looking at them and criticising them for not being able to care for their own kids. Jane is always very kind to all the children's parents. She went with me a few times when I visited my mum and she didn't mind when my mum mistook us for someone else and started to scream. But I did, and that's why I hardly ever see my mum these days.)

I asked Donald again whether there's any way that Ryan could move in with Jane and Martin (so when the time is right he could move into the flat I'll have). But I knew what the answer was going to be. The real problem is that Ryan and I don't have the same dads.

My mum was married to my dad but they were always rowing and leaving each other, then getting back together. One time when they first split up, she met this other man and got pregnant with Ryan. Then my parents got back together again for a bit and everyone pretended that me and Ryan had the same dad. Even I thought Ryan was my full-brother for ages. But after the marriage went totally wrong my mum got in touch with Ryan's dad again – she introduced us to him as "Uncle David" and we couldn't work out why we'd never met him before. Though she insisted I'd met him when I was younger, I had no memory of it.

I don't think this David's ever been much use or anything because he never seemed to keep a job, and he didn't stick around with Mum when she needed him. And he never seemed that interested in seeing Ryan, as far as I could tell. But his sister started to come and visit us and bring her mother along – and she told us that she was Ryan's grandmother. So when Mum was taken into hospital and my dad left, the aunt and grandmother asked if they could have Ryan to live with them. But they didn't want me.

And everyone completely seemed to forget that Ryan thought my dad was his dad for all those years and would rather they'd made more effort to keep us both in touch with him, even if he was in America.

Ryan lived with the aunt and grandmother until he got to about ten, when they discovered that looking after boys isn't as easy as they'd thought. They were very religious and they started beating him because he wouldn't do the things they thought he should. So then the social workers decided he couldn't live with them all the time and they moved him to foster carers nearby, who could "maintain his links with his birth family". But nobody seemed to remember I'm more his family than any of them; I'm his sister and I've been with him since he was born. I looked after him for years when Mum was ill. And I'll be there for him when he's grown up and all those other relatives are all dead and gone.

Ryan has told me that his aunt and grandmother hardly ever visit him any more and he's not seen his birth dad for about a year. He says that Kitty and Craig aren't very welcoming to them when they visit, so he doesn't blame them for not wanting to come to the house. He's not allowed to go to visit them because they used to beat him but Ryan says he doesn't think they'd do that now. Besides he's 13 and big enough to fight back if they tried anything like that.

Ryan says that most of all he wants to be with me, and he has this mad idea that if the two of us could get to my dad's place in America, then we could all live together. He saw something in a film and he thinks that in America the laws are much simpler. But that's wrong – the USA has really tough immigration rules. And besides, if my dad wanted me he'd have been in touch years ago.

I read in one of Jane's books about fostering that, wherever possible, children should grow up with their brothers and sisters. I just wish someone would tell that to the people who make all the decisions for Ryan and me. I've tried to – but they never listen.

Kitty came out to meet us as soon as Donald's car pulled up in her driveway. She was looking really stressed. Good, I thought, she's come to tell Donald that she can't cope with Ryan any more and he'll have to be moved immediately. Then I could suggest that he came back to Jane and Martin's with me – just for the moment.

But when I got out of the car, Kitty came straight up to me and attempted to hug me. 'Ryan'll be so pleased yoose come,' she said in that funny accent of hers. She's a tiny little woman with a long blonde plait hanging down her back, except it's getting a bit grey in places. 'We've been that worried about him.'

I remember that I actually liked Kitty quite a lot when I first met her. She has fierce, darting eyes which are never still for a moment – like she can see round corners. She's always cracking jokes and she's got a very positive outlook on life, which reminds me of myself. Craig, however, I've never been sure about. He's the strong, silent type. He's ex-navy and very matter of fact and Ryan says he's as stubborn as you can get. Which I suppose is a bit rich coming from Ryan who's the most stubborn person I ever met.

I gave Kitty a bit of a stiff hug back but she didn't seem to notice. 'Come in pet,' she said 'you must be tired after that long journey,' and she took my overnight bag out of my hand and carried it herself.

Kitty had set out a big plate of "butties" and cake for me in the front room. She told me Ryan was in his bedroom, probably playing on the computer. She said I'd probably best go up and see him as he'd been refusing to come downstairs since he got back from the hospital. I said I'd like to talk to her before I saw Ryan, and Donald said that this might be a good moment for him to pop up and see Ryan himself.

I told Kitty that I thought it would be so much better if Ryan could come and live near me. That I knew my foster carers would have him. I'd probably told her this before but she'd never seemed to listen properly. Today she said, 'Sure pet, you're probably right. But Ryan's family won't allow that. I've tried to talk to them about it – told them Ryan should be moved near to you. That he frets to be with his sister all the time.'

I could hardly believe what I was hearing. It seemed the situation had got really complicated and Ryan didn't know the half of it.

Kitty then told me that Ryan's aunt and grandmother nearly exploded when she tried to talk to them about Ryan's feelings. They told her that the court was on their side and they had rights to see Ryan whenever they wanted. 'The last time they came round here, pet, there was this awful atmosphere and they wouldn't speak to me no' any of the children. And they didn't come to see Ryan, just moan about the council taking Ryan away in the first place. I'm afraid I lost my rag and told them not to bother coming here again coz it wasn't doing Ryan any favours. And they made no end of fuss to the social workers. If it wasn't for Donald, they'd have took Ryan off us straight away and sent him to some emergency foster carers. Ryan may not like us much but he's best here for the time being – till he can be with you.'

I told Ryan all of this when I went upstairs to see him. He was just staring at the computer screen, stabbing the keyboard. Killing somebody or something that I couldn't see properly coz the table lamp was reflected in the screen. He'd got the curtains shut tight in his bedroom, even though it was a brilliant summer's day outside.

My brother looked up when I arrived, but didn't move. The swellings round his eyes had started coming out properly now – all mauve and green and black like some kind of camouflage. I suspected that was why he didn't want to come out of his room, coz he was embarrassed about the way he looked. I went and stood behind him and kissed him on the top of his head. I put my hands on his shoulders and just stood there for a while, although he didn't seem to be paying any attention to me.

'Aren't you pleased to see me?' I asked him eventually.

'Yeah, it's good to see you sis.' But he said it in such a dull, almost sarcastic voice that it was hard to know if he meant it.

'I've just had an amazing conversation with Kitty. Did you know she'd told your so-called family that she thought you should come back to live near me?'

Ryan shrugged. 'Whatever,' he said. 'That woman will say anything.'

'Yeah, but I honestly think she meant it,' I told Ryan. 'I can see through people and I don't think she's lying.'

'Probably coz she's sick of having me here now. They wants rid of me,' my brother said, continuing to stare straight ahead into a virtual world that seemed much more important than anything I could say to him.

'I know she can be pig-headed and all that...and I don't like Craig that much if I'm honest, but I get the impression that they do care what happens to you. They're prepared to have you here until they can persuade social services to let you come back to live near me. Just think, you might be able to come and live at Jane and Martin's!'

A week ago Ryan would have jumped at this idea, but he wasn't reacting at all. I started to feel worried. 'Ryan! Did you hear what I just said? I thought that was what you wanted?'

'Whatever.'

I had to stop myself shaking my brother. 'OK,' I said, 'I'm going to unpack my bag now. Shall I see you downstairs at tea?'

My brother just shrugged. And he didn't appear for tea – which Kitty said had been the pattern for several days. So she put food on a tray and I ate mine with him in his room. Ryan didn't eat much but just kept playing the computer game, never taking his eyes away from the screen. I tried to keep talking to him – about all the things I'd been doing since I saw him a few days ago at the hospital.

I told Ryan about the things I'd been buying for my new room, and the curtains Jane was helping me make. But Ryan's a boy and I suspect that wouldn't interest him much, even at the best of times. I also told him about my plan to get a sofa-bed from Sean's uncle, so he could come and stay. And how Sean's dad has offered to lend Sean one of his trucks from work so he can pick it up for me. (I didn't tell Ryan about the row I'd had with Sean and how he didn't speak to me again till he heard the news that Ryan was in hospital. Then he came round with a big bunch of flowers for me. And that's when he told me he'd found a dead cheap but mint sofa-bed for me. I guess he thinks he'll be invited to sleep on it. But I'll deal with that one when I get to it.)

I used up all my news but still Ryan didn't say anything. In the end I said I'd take the dishes downstairs and give a hand with the washing up. Kitty asked me how Ryan seemed and I just raised my eyebrows at her. She said I should try not to worry too much; my brother had been pretty shaken up by getting beaten up and shock could do funny things to people. Or that's what the doctor had told her when she rang him to talk about her concerns. But she assured me she would demand that the doctor came to visit if he wasn't any better in a day or two.

Kitty and I – and the other foster kid, Lewis – watched a DVD together. I tried to get Ryan to come down, but he said he'd already seen it. I asked if he wanted me to sit with him but he said he didn't, so I went back downstairs.

Craig came in about 10.30. He'd been out at the Territorial Army – probably shouting at small boys or whatever it is those people do. He was quite civil to me and said it was nice to see me. He never says that normally so I went to bed really worried that something was definitely up with Ryan.

On the Saturday, I was planning to take Ryan into the city. We usually go bowling and then I take him for a burger or something. It shows that social workers trust me coz for the last couple of years they've let me take my brother out on my own; they never worry about me trying to kidnap him or anything like that. But when I went in to check on Ryan on Saturday morning he was lying with the duvet pulled up over his head. It was only ten o'clock and I guess some kids like to lie in, so I told him I'd be back to find him in half an hour. But he was still in bed when I checked him again. So I said I'd be back at 11. But at 11 he was just staring at the ceiling, not doing anything. 'C'mon Ryan – get out of bed,' I said, starting to pull the duvet away from him. 'You can't stay there all day.'

Normally he'd have yelled at me and tried to pull back the duvet but he just let me pull it away from him. Then he curled up into a tight little ball with his arms over his head. Like one of those pictures of babies curled up in the womb. 'Ryan, you're really freaking me out,' I said, 'Please talk to me. Say something. Say anything.' But he just continued to lie there, motionless.

I went downstairs to tell Kitty. Kitty put her arm round me and I think I cried a bit onto her shoulder. She went upstairs herself then and I made myself some more tea. I couldn't eat anything that morning, even though Lewis was tucking into a big plate of fried food. 'Second breakfast,' he told me proudly. 'I had cereal and juice at half past eight. But I did football practice with Craig in the garden and it wore me out.'

I think Lewis is about 15 but he had some kind of brain damage when he was a baby. He acts like a much younger kid, but he's kind and gentle most of the time. Sometimes he gets a bit wound up by little things and he flies off into a temper, but most of the time he's nice enough to have around. I talked to Lewis about fish, which is his favourite subject. He has a tank of tropical fish in his bedroom, which Craig installed last Christmas. He knows the name of every type of fish and he told me in great detail about each one. I tried not to worry about Ryan but I kept listening out for Kitty's footsteps on the stairs. She seemed to have been upstairs for a long time.

Kitty came down eventually. She beckoned me into the hallway. 'He still won't talk to me, pet. I'm going to call the doctor,' she told me. 'Just to be on the safe side. It's probably just coz of the shock – it can take people in funny ways.'

I went up to Ryan's room and talked to him. 'Look little brother,' I said. 'This is crunch time. If you really are that depressed then you need help and the doctor will probably decide you should go to hospital, and they'll give you drugs and counselling and things. But if you're putting this on to get our attention then it's probably not a good idea.'

Ryan sat up suddenly. 'Why do women fuss so much?' he said. 'It was just a headache. It's gone now.'

I felt a wave of relief, but I wasn't going to let my brother off the hook so easily. 'You could have said that earlier, instead of all the silent drama queen stuff.'

'My head was hurting something awful. An' I was seeing stars and feeling that sick I'd probably have thrown up all over you if I was talking.'

I wasn't totally convinced but I was relieved that my brother was talking again. 'I'll tell Kitty to cancel the doctor's visit – if it's not already too late.'

But Kitty was still waiting to get through to the weekend emergency service. She seemed relieved when I told her that Ryan was talking now – and claiming he'd had a headache. 'He's had them before,' she said. 'Oh well, if he says he feels better now then I don't think we should fret too much. I'll just keep an eye on him, pet – and talk to Donald on Monday.'

Ten minutes later Ryan appeared downstairs, dressed and

looking almost presentable. He wolfed down two bowls of Coco Pops and then asked me, 'Are we going into town now?'

I raised my eyebrows at Kitty, who nodded. 'I could run yoose up to the bowling centre...'

But Ryan said he wanted to go to a film. And Lewis immediately said he wanted to see it too. As Ryan didn't seem to mind, Kitty said it was fine if I took them both. (And she gave me a £20 note to pay for their tickets.) It wasn't something I was crazy about seeing, but my 13-year-old brother and a very excitable Lewis – who made a lot of noise – spent the afternoon happily watching stupid men with guns chasing each other in a random mix of cars, motorbikes, HGVs and speedboats. A lot of extras got blown up or drove off the road, but none of the main characters seemed to suffer anything more than a scratch to their paintwork. At the end somebody got the money and somebody else got the blonde girl with big bosoms and no brains, but if there was any real storyline I certainly couldn't follow it. Instead I spent most of the time making lists in my head about all the things I still needed to do for my move. Which is only five days away.

Ryan seemed fine for the rest of the day – he even ate tea with everyone else and helped Lewis describe the film to Craig. But then something happened last night which totally freaked me out.

I was just passing my brother's bedroom door when I heard whispers. Except one of the people whispering was Lewis who's not very good at it. I could hear him saying over and over again, 'You got to give it back Ryan. It's a sin!'

Ryan was trying to shush him, but it wasn't working. So I let myself into the room.

'What's going on?' I demanded.

Both boys turned round to stare at me. Lewis's eyes were full of fear but Ryan had a defiant look on his face which I didn't like.

'OK,' I said. 'Tell me what's happening.'

'Nothing,' Ryan looked me full in the eyes, daring me to challenge him further.

'Doesn't look like nothing,' I said.

At this point Lewis burst into tears. 'It's OK, Lewis,' I said drawing him towards me, with my hand on his arm. 'D' you want me to get Kitty?'

'No!' Ryan jumped up from the chair where he'd been sitting. 'You can't do that.'

'Then you'd better explain – quick.'

But Ryan stood there silently. And I started wondering what the heck I was going to do.

'He took the lady's purse – and it's a sin,' Lewis blurted out suddenly.

I watched my brother's face flush scarlet. 'Yeah, and so what,' he turned to face the trembling Lewis. 'My sister won't care. She used to shoplift all the time when she was my age.'

'You little liar!' I was so furious I found myself grabbing Ryan by the shoulders. I wanted to shake him till his teeth fell out. 'I've never stolen anything in my life...OK maybe some Starbursts from a shop when I was eleven and I did it for a stupid dare – but I wouldn't steal anything that belonged to someone. And if you've stolen something, then you'd better give it back – or I'm calling the police.'

'You'd call the cops? On your little bruvver? I thought you were cooler than that, sis. I'm disappointed in you.' Ryan glared at me, his eyes narrow with contempt.

'Yes – I would! Some poor person is probably going mental. That could be the only money they have to live on. For weeks.'

'Stealing is wrong. My teacher told me, and my nana says so,' An anxious Lewis, who I'd almost forgotten about, piped up from behind me.

'Nah, she looked rich enough. She won't miss it,' Ryan was

smiling now and I had to force myself not to slap him.

'How can you tell?' I demanded.

'She had posh clothes and these fancy earrings – I think they were diamonds...she was that one sitting next to us in the cinema. She was with her mates, all dressed up they were. Bet she's got a rich boyfriend or something...'

'And that Traveller girl you used to play with at the kids centre had diamond earrings but it didn't mean she was rich...Besides, that's not the point. You can't go around stealing other people's stuff. That's not the way Mum brought us up. Show me what you've taken.'

'When did you get to become such a saint?' Ryan glared at me, his arms folded across his chest.

'Give it to me now – or I'm calling Craig and Kitty,' I told him. I didn't really intend to do this, but I could tell that Ryan was taking me seriously.

'Fine, if it stops you nagging,' Ryan had that infuriating smile back on his face. 'You know you're getting like Mum...nag, nag nag...all the time,' my brother turned his back on me and got something out of a drawer. He handed me a white leather purse with a gold-coloured clasp.

'You won't find much in there sis,' he said, his voice low and mocking. 'Just a few pounds. But you're welcome to keep it if it makes you feel better.'

The first thing I saw inside the purse was a photograph of a baby. (A very ugly baby in my opinion but I'm not much of a baby person.) Then there was a bus pass and also a couple of credit cards and some store loyalty cards, and a ten-pound note.

'Nope – no receipts for yachts or mink coats here,' I told Ryan. 'Just a lot of receipts for nappies and bread and stuff. Seems that woman was some poor mum having time out to herself which my stupid brother ruined for her.'

'Aw, come on sis, you're being daft...' Ryan still had a really irritating smile on his face.

'Shall we call the police?' Lewis volunteered.

Ryan stepped forward menacingly and I thought he was about to thump Lewis. Instead he said, 'Shut up, you stupid baby.'

'Ryan! That's enough!' I was fed up with my brother's pathetic behaviour. 'You know Lewis's idea's not a bad one. You nick some poor woman's purse and then you think it's funny or something...'

'Shall we call the police?' Lewis asked, from where he was hiding behind me. 'We have to dial 999.'

'No, Lewis,' I said, trying to sound calmer than I felt. 'It's alright, I will deal with this. I think we all need to calm down and get some sleep. And Ryan...' I fixed my little brother with the coldest stare I could imagine, 'You better do some hard thinking before the morning. About what we're gonna do about this purse.'

'Like what?' Ryan scowled, his arms crossed over his chest.

'Like taking it into a police station and saying you found it or posting it to the woman who owns it, or whatever. Otherwise I'm going to have to tell Kitty and Craig about this.'

'We have to tell Craig and Kitty!' Lewis insisted urgently, still sheltering behind me. 'We have to tell them secrets because otherwise secrets can hurt people.'

Someone had done horrible things to Lewis when he was a little kid and told him it was just "their secret" and he must never tell anyone. It was years before anyone realised what was happening and only after the person who was abusing Lewis was caught hurting another child. So I knew why Kitty and Craig made a big thing of telling Lewis that secrets could hurt people. But I was really scared what might happen if someone realised that my brother had actually started nicking things. I didn't think they'd put him in a young offenders' institute for a first offence, but I wasn't taking any risks.

'It's OK,' I told Lewis, lying through my teeth, 'You don't have to worry about *this* secret. This isn't *your* secret. I will tell Kitty and Craig about it, so you can forget about it completely.'

I could feel Lewis's terrible uncertainty. I took his hand, steering him gently towards the door. 'It really is OK,' I reassured him. 'This is an adult problem and I'm an adult now. It's my job to sort it out.'

I wanted to do something stupid like make Lewis promise he wouldn't talk about this to anyone, but I knew that would be so unfair on him. I just had to hope he'd take my word for it and forget about it. He did that sometimes, particularly when he got distracted by something new. 'Will you play football in the garden tomorrow?' I asked, hoping that this might do the trick.

Lewis brightened up instantly. 'No,' he told me firmly. 'Me and Craig are going to the fish shop.'

Then Lewis wanted to show me his fish tank all over again – although he'd shown it to me already that day. I was just leaving his room when Kitty appeared on the landing. 'Everything OK?' she asked, a bit puzzled as to what I was doing in Lewis's room.

'Yes, fine,' I told her breezily. 'I found Lewis in Ryan's room – they were squabbling about something silly and I took Lewis back to his bedroom. Then of course, he wanted me to show me his fish again...'

'Ah Holly, you're such a sensible lass,' Kitty patted me on the arm. 'Why are lassies always so much more mature than boys?'

Why did I feel so guilty then? I knew I had to look after my brother but lying to Kitty felt wrong. And lying to Lewis was even worse. But I went back to my bedroom telling myself that no harm would come to anyone. It wasn't Lewis's secret and he wouldn't get hurt by it in any way.

I tried to speak to my brother again, but he refused to answer when I knocked softly on his door. I opened it slightly but the light was out and he seemed to be huddled under the duvet. 'Sleep well,' I said softly. 'You're a bad lad Ryan, but I do still love you. You're my little brother and I will always love you. We'll have a proper talk in the morning.'

The figure under the duvet moved and mumbled something. I tried to convince myself he'd said 'Love you too, sis' but I really couldn't be sure.

Ryan disappeared before breakfast. Kitty and I were both late risers and it wasn't until we'd finished our tea and toast that I decided to go up and give my brother a wake-up call. There was a duvet heaped up in the bed to look like a body shape, but it wasn't very convincing. I ran downstairs to tell Kitty, who said he'd possibly gone out early with Craig and Lewis to the pet shop, but I think we both knew that wasn't likely. Craig had forgotten his mobile so Kitty couldn't check. She started making Sunday dinner so I gave her a hand. We both needed something to keep us busy.

After what seemed like forever, Lewis came into the kitchen beaming and carefully carrying a polythene bag with a tiny, jewel-like fish darting around in the water inside it. But neither Lewis nor Craig had seen Ryan that morning. I tried to pretend an interest in the little fish to keep Lewis occupied, while Craig and Kitty decided on a plan of action. I heard Craig phoning Donald on his mobile, while Kitty and I laid the table and tried to decide whether to set a place for Ryan or not.

We were just sitting down to eat when Donald arrived. Lewis kept asking over and over again where Ryan was – because he wanted Ryan to see his new fish – and Craig and Kitty and Donald had to keep telling him that they really didn't know, but hoped he'd be back in time for tea. I had this huge worry that Lewis might mention the stolen purse, but he seemed to have forgotten all about it. Lewis is someone who lives in the moment. Sometimes I wish my life was that simple.

Anyway, Donald said we shouldn't fret too much. Ryan is

probably 'asserting his independence after the recent attack, and will be back soon'. (He said this through a mouthful of roast potatoes – Kitty had insisted he ate Ryan's dinner and he seemed happy enough about this. I wonder about Donald sometimes. Does that man have a life?)

Donald said I should go back to Jane and Martin's as planned. He knew this was the week of my big move and he couldn't see any point in me hanging around. Kitty made it clear that I was welcome to stay as long as I liked, and even Craig said the same. You could tell he was really cut up about Ryan. Maybe he's not such a bad person after all.

After a cup of tea, I packed my bags and Donald offered to run me to the station. (He definitely doesn't have a life.) He asked me some questions on the way – about anything I'd noticed about Ryan during the weekend. I told him about Ryan's mood swings but I don't tell him about the purse. I wouldn't have anyone thinking that my little brother was a criminal.

The train was delayed and I told Donald not to wait coz I wanted to choose some magazines for the journey. As soon as he left, I went to the lost property office.

'I found this in the ladies toilet,' I told the bored looking bloke behind the desk, who was eating his tea.

'There's a bus pass and credit card in there and you should be able to trace the person through their bank, or something. You'll make sure they get it, won't you? I'd be in bits if I'd lost my purse.'

'Sure, love. You want to leave your address in case they want to give you a reward or summat?'

I wasn't sure if the guy meant that or was just winding me up. I said that I didn't.

'Virtue its own reward, then, with you luv?' He positively leered at me from behind a ham sandwich, and I left quickly.

Lucy and Martin were waiting for me at Corrington station.

They were standing behind the barrier and Lucy started jumping and waving as soon as I stepped off the train. She flung her arms around me the minute I was close enough. It was nice to be back but that was a bit over the top. Maybe she thought that now Ryan's gone missing I will postpone moving out. But I won't. She should know me better by now.

WEDNESDAY 5 AUGUST
(Day one of Going it Alone)

10pm

At last – the first night in my own place. Well, sort of. At least it's my own room with all my own stuff around me. Jane and Lucy helped me move all my stuff here and unpack some of it, but then they tried to persuade me to leave some of the boxes till tomorrow. Jane said I looked tired. I said, 'OK,' I'd leave it till tomorrow, but as soon as I'd packed them off with a cup of tea and a quick introduction to Nathan (who wandered in clutching a football DVD but then did a double-take when he saw Lucy's cute bod), I unpacked the last of my boxes.

I'd been determined not to cry when I left the house – I'll be seeing them all again soon. But as I unpacked, I kept remembering the sad look on the face of the new boy (I still can't remember if he's called Steven or Simon) when he watched Martin loading my stuff into the back of the people carrier. But I really don't have time to worry about him coz I've got my own brother to worry about. Anyway this day was meant to be about me and the start of my new life.

But my eyes did get a bit watery when I found a lump under my duvet. It was Lucy's Mr Giraffe with a label round its neck.

Love ya Holly-bolly! I want him back when he gets homesick :)
L xxx

Silly girl. She knows I don't do stuffed animals. But it was a dead sweet thought. I sent her a text saying, *Hiya Lucy-Poocy. Thanx 4 Mr G. He mightee fine company. Luv ya too :)*

I wondered about telling her that Nathan asked about her. But I decided to wait until next time Dreadful Daniel is mean to her and Lucy starts crying and saying she's fat and ugly. (Lucy tells me that she and DD are all loved up again, so I'm keeping my nose out of it for now. At least she hasn't said anything more about being "late", so I guess that's one thing I don't need to worry about.)

It happened while I was cooking spag bol (Martin's secret recipe). Nathan appeared in the kitchen, sniffing the air like a starving wolf. I guessed he'd turn up so I'd made loads. 'You're welcome to eat with me,' I told him, 'but you've got to wash up afterwards. That's the deal.'

Which reminds me that tomorrow I must talk to Nathan about some kind of house rota. If we have a kitty for food and household things, it will work out cheaper and he'll get decent meals. I can write the shopping lists and he can go down to the shops and carry it back. (All those biceps have to be good for something.) Then I'll do the cooking and the more difficult bits of housework, like keeping the bathroom properly clean and defrosting the fridge. And Nathan can do all the easy bits like vacuuming and dusting, and putting out the bins.

Nathan wanted us to watch TV while we ate but I said that we should talk to each other. He looked at me like I'd just stepped out of a spaceship and had my ears on my bum. Naturally he was happy to talk once I started asking him questions about football (Jane always does that with people who are a bit shy. She finds something they really like and then pretends that she's really interested and starts to ask them all these questions about it.

It works every time.) I don't care that much about football myself
– I've moved around too much to support any team properly – but
I like playing footie, and I'll watch a match if it's on the telly. But I
guess I'll soon be an expert if I live here for long enough.

After we finished, Nathan did the dishes (not very well. Why
do boys always think it's OK just to hold plates under the hot tap?).
While he was sloshing water around he asked me, quite casually:
'Dat blonde girl, what's she called? She into football?' I told him
Lucy's name, but that he'd have to ask her himself about football.
(As far as I'm aware Lucy tends to support whichever team her
current boyfriend supports, but I didn't think this was a good thing
to tell Nathan.)

'Girls!' Nathan snorted, raising a single eyebrow. 'They never
know important stuff about their mates. What colour lipstick she
wear, now dat is different...'

I used this as a cue to ask Nathan about his sister, Keesha, who
I still haven't seen.

'Man, my sister is some crazy chick!' Nathan said shaking his
head. 'She and that Mel, they just want to party, party, party. They
woke me so many nights I cuss them. That's when Keesh said I was
stinkin' the place out wiv my kit.'

I was a bit worried hearing that. I like to party myself but not
every night, especially when I've got to study. 'Don't Phil and Cathy
say anything to her?' I asked, genuinely curious. I thought that part
of "learning to be independent" was learning how to get a proper
balance in your life. You've got to weigh it up, like putting things on
the scale, that's what one of my other foster carers used to say. For
every bit of hard work there's a bit of fun and the other way round.
Too much of one and the scales get out of balance. She talked a
load of rubbish that foster carer, but that was one thing I did agree
with.

Nathan shrugged. 'Cath don't come round much since she got

her new job. Wasn't meant to be full time, but she say she feels like someone pulling her in too many ways. She's a nice lady – don't get me wrong – but she's always busy-busy. Some days, Phil come round in the mornings and sit in his office. His door always open but he don't come out of it much. He says he's "drownin' in paperwork" and him always on dat phone. He's one busy man. Serious.'

I know about social workers like that. That's why so many of them burn out or give up or have a nervous breakdown. If they're any good at their job, their boss asks them to do everyone else's job as well, coz everyone else is on sick leave or maternity leave or has run away to join the navy. Or something like that. Then there are all the systems they are supposed to manage. Ahmina pretends she's cool with it all, but I always see piles and piles of paper in her in-tray and she looks half terrified every time she has to switch on her computer. I offered once to help her tidy everything up and make a proper filing system. She said it was nice of me, but there were "confidentiality issues" to consider.

Which reminds me – I haven't heard from Ahmina yet. As my leaving care worker, she should be checking I'm doing OK. Some leaving care workers – well, the good ones – help young people move in. Ahmina did send me a card, and she said she knew I was 'in very good hands with Jane and Martin' and I should call her if I needed anything. And she made some feeble excuse about being tied up with 'personal issues'. But that isn't the point.

I think it's time I went to sleep. It's almost 11pm and I'm supposed to be getting up early. I'm going to send one more text to Ryan. This time I'm going to cut the softly softly stuff and tell him how incredibly angry I am with him, coz everyone is worried sick...

It's sent now. Maybe it was a bit strong, but he needs to know how we all feel about this. And I wonder if it was a good idea to include my new address. Is he going to see that as like some kind of invitation to come here? I just don't know. I thought I knew my little brother but I haven't a clue any more. Enough. I need to get some shut-eye.

Goodnight new bedroom, I hope we are going to get on.

Midnight

I'm so cross and I can't sleep now. Sean rang just as I was nodding off to say he hadn't heard from me and wondered if I was OK. He said he'd been texting me all day. I was really quite snappy with him. Doesn't he know how much I've had to do? Then he started going on about how he'll deliver that sofa-bed tomorrow afternoon. I told him I'd rather he came round in the morning because I have things to do in the afternoon. He said he couldn't do that coz he had to take one of his dad's other vans in for a service. I said surely this could wait another day and he said it couldn't. In the end we agreed that he'd come round in the evening, and he said, 'You can buy me a drink afterwards!' and then I hit the roof. I told him I have no spare money to waste on going to the pub and if he wants to celebrate my new place then maybe he should think about bringing a bottle round here. (His mum and dad's wine rack is always full, I bet he can ask them for one.)

Then Sean said, 'Sometimes Holly you are so tight I can't believe you!' I think he meant it as a kind of a joke but I didn't think it was funny. Sean's parents buy everything for him – well at least they are paying for his university and they paid for his holiday last year. He says they are making him pay his own way now, as they think he needs to be as independent as possible before he leaves home. But I think that's a load of rubbish. If Sean got in debt or anything, he could still go back to his parents and ask for help. Who could I go to? So I need every penny I've got to invest in my future.

He must have realised I was mad coz after a few moment of

silence, he said, 'C'mon Holly, don't be like that. You know how I feel about you. It's just sometimes I feel that all you want me for is for me to do things for you – you never give me anything back.'

Great. Now he's back to the fact that I won't sleep with him. I disconnected the phone, and switched off the ring tone. Because if he's going to be like that I don't want anything more to do with him. Stuff him and his uncle's stupid sofa-bed; it would probably be really manky anyway. All that family seem to be greedy losers.

THURSDAY 6 AUGUST
Day 2 of Going It Alone

Midday

Today was a normal sort of day. To start with at least. I finished tidying up my bits and pieces, and then I had a proper look round. We don't have a washing machine in our flat but there's a couple of big ones in the basement, and a tumble dryer. They take 50p coins so I need to start a jar to collect them. And the hoover in our place is really rubbish. So I went out to the shops to get some stuff. I checked my bank account and it was looking OK, so I got a pretty decent vacuum from Tesco's. They had some on special offer and they came with a two-year guarantee. I never buy electrical stuff from market stalls coz you don't know what you're getting, but that doesn't mean you have to go to one of the posh electricity shops. You just have to hunt around a bit and get a bargain. I also got a drying frame for my bedroom so I don't have to use the tumble dryer that much.

Then I bought myself something to celebrate. It was crazy really coz I was staggering along to the bus stop with a great big rectangular box under one arm and a long flat box under the other, when I saw them. The most awesome pair of boots I've ever seen. They were that bright red colour you get on Christmas cards – the colour of Rudolph's nose or Santa's jacket. And they were dead shiny. They were ankle boots with this spike heel and then all these strappy bits and buckles. And they were jumping up and down in the window and calling out my name.

I was going to walk past. It was my first full day in my new place and I wasn't going to be one of those care leavers who fritters all their money on clothes and having a good time, and then has nothing left to pay for bills and household stuff. But the fact was that these weren't just my most perfect pair of boots ever, they were also in a closing down sale. They'd been reduced from £99 to £37. And they did look like they were good quality. I won't spend my money on tatty junk that falls apart the second time you wear it. The stuff I buy has got to last.

Anyway I thought, they probably won't have them in my size (I have really big feet coz I'm tall) or they'll pinch my toes or something. But 20 minutes later I was walking out of the shop with a carrier bag as well as the boxes, and I felt like the cat who got the canary.

In the afternoon I took a wander over to the college to see how far it is from my place. It's hardly any distance at all, so apart from really wet days I can easily walk it in 15 minutes. I still have to get Ahmina to apply for some funding for me for things like travel. The local authority has to pay for your living accommodation till you're 18 but they should also pay for most of your college expenses. Of course some of them try to wriggle off the hook, and are really cheap about it, but I told Ahmina that I will get in touch with the council if they don't pay me what I'm due. Ahmina laughed and said it was the councillors who'd made all the cutbacks so I should blame them if there wasn't much money for extra things. But I suspect she's just fobbing me off, as she's probably too scared to stand up to the people in the finance department. I may have to go and see that Winston again if things don't turn out right.

I hate to admit it but I was so knackered when I got home (and I didn't exactly get much sleep last night) that I had a little snooze on my bed. But not till after I'd tried out the new vacuum, which works a treat. I was thinking that maybe I'd call Sean this evening and try and make up because I saw the price of sofa-beds in Argos and it was megabuck-city! Anyway, I kind of miss having Sean to talk to. Then I must have drifted off or something…

I had the weirdest dream! The phone was ringing and I knew it was Ryan trying to call me. I also knew that my phone was inside the box that the vacuum came in, which I'd squashed down and put into the recycling bin by the front door. So I was trying to get the box out of the bin but as I leaned over the bin I fell in. And I realised that it wasn't a bin at all but at the bottom there was a trapdoor that led to a secret passageway – like a chute. And it came out into these underground caves.

There were little lights all around the caves, like torches or lanterns, and when I'd dusted myself down I went to have a closer look. There were children sitting in the caves, huddled round the candles. One of the children I recognised as the new boy from Jane and Martin's. And he looked at me with his big sad eyes but he didn't say anything. Then I knew that Ryan was there somewhere, and I just had to find him. So I took out my phone (which somehow was now back in my jeans pocket) and I dialled his number, and the phone went on ringing and ringing and I knew Ryan was listening to it and deciding whether he was going to answer.

I woke up to find that my mobile really was ringing – to let me know about a whole series of missed calls. Sean had called to say that as I obviously didn't want the sofa-bed delivering, he'd taken another job for his dad this afternoon. Maybe I would "deign" to speak to him later. (He irritates me when he uses stupid words.)

No I won't "deign" to speak him later. Let him stew for another day.

Jane had called to say she hoped I'd settled in OK, and she was really sorry that she hadn't been in touch earlier but that the new boy (apparently his name really is Simon) had been rushed into hospital in the middle of the night, so she'd been rather tied up all day. (She reassured me in the message that he was doing OK, although it had a bit worrying at the time. I know she can't tell me more coz info about other foster kids is confidential, but it's hard when they are living as part of your family. You don't mean to, but you worry about them all the same. Maybe she'll tell me more when I see her at the weekend.)

And the last message was a missed call. From Ryan – just his mobile number, nothing more. No message or anything to say where he was. I was so angry with myself for not picking up his call that I burst into tears.

I was making tea in the kitchen when the door to the hall opened. I could hear girls' voices and the sound of Nathan's steady, muscle-bound step. The voices headed into the living room so I immediately found an excuse to go out to the hallway and sure enough – the living room door was open. And sitting on the couch was one of the most stunning girls I'd even seen. A curvier version of Nathan, with his lazy, handsome features turned into the most beautiful pouting mouth and turned up nose. She had bright pink and silver hair cut into a bob that rested just above her shoulders (I think it was a wig) and was wearing a cute little silver jacket and the tightest pair of stretch black jeans. Over these she wore a thigh-high pair of patent black boots, with heels even higher than the ones I'd bought that morning. She wasn't what you'd ever call skinny but she looked so good you just wanted to be her. And she was chatting away, waving her hands around, so full of life. Her wrists were covered in silver bangles which jangled and shimmied as she moved. I almost forgave the fact she was holding a lit cigarette.

'Hey!' I said sliding in at the door. 'You must be Keesha?'

'You bet I must!' the bird of paradise replied, resting her head back against the sofa and laughing, a deep gravelly laugh. 'And you hun, must be Saint Holly. Anyone who puts up wiv my likkle bruvver – she's a big saint in my book.' And she laughed again, bracelets tinkling and earrings as big as chandeliers swinging alongside her perfectly chiselled cheekbones.

'Come sit down, sugar. We need to know all about you, girl!'

Keesha patted the sofa between them. The other girl, who was white, and almost as startling as Keesha, shifted up a bit so I could sit down. She had the palest skin and black-mauve spikey-cut hair. She was dressed all in black, and most of it was leather.

'I'm Mel,' she said. Not quite as welcoming as Keesha.

'Ain't you just gorg-e-o-u-s!' Keesha says after looking me up and down. 'Me and Mel know this guy who has this hot model agency, and you, girl, have just the kind of legs and fine looks those model agency people goes crazy over. We should introduce you.'

'Yeah, we get a bonus if we bring in new talent,' Mel said a bit off-handedly from behind a wreath of smoke. I got the impression Mel is used to being the centre of Keesha's attention and was a bit antsy that I'd turned up. This was exactly the sort of situation I didn't want to get into.

I shook my head. 'Thanks but I'm nowhere like as fine as you two. You're both amazing.' (See, I can be a diplomat when I try. Jane would be very proud of me.) 'Anyway, I've got my art course to concentrate on.'

Keesha laughed again. 'Hey hun, that's just college stuff. No one bothers much about that. Mel's doing textile design and I'm doing hospitality, but we don't go in much. And anyway girl, it ain't term time yet! Plenty of time to go a likkle bit crazeee! Don't you get like my bruvver here. He so obsessed with dat sports course he doing, he don't fink of nothing else.'

Nathan grunted but the atmosphere between them seemed to be a lot friendlier than I'd expected. He watched his sister with a sort of amused tolerance, and occasionally stole a glance at me. I guess she's a pretty amazing sister to have and he's probably used to strangers being blown away by her.

I ended up showing Keesha and Mel the boots I'd bought earlier. They were full of admiration. 'Just fine for that party we're having tonight!' Keesha told me. 'We must of known you was buying them.'

Mel said at this point that they really ought to go downstairs and start getting ready. And Keesha said that that reminded her that they hadn't come on a purely social visit. They wanted to borrow the flat hoover – even if it was a bit clapped out. 'That mate of Saul's – whatssisface – broke ours. He tried to hoover these broken glasses up...' Mel explained.

I was about to wonder if I should quickly hide my new vacuum cleaner before anyone saw it, but the mention of Saul's friend stopped me. And I started wondering if maybe this was that bloke who'd let me in the first time I came round.

'Hey, don't you come whatsafacein' with me, my girl!' Keesha wagged her finger at Mel. 'We all know you fancy dat Tol-mee guy.'

Bingo! It was Mr Green Eyes.

But Mel tossed her head at Keesha's remark. 'You must be joking! That bloke's a loser. I wouldn't touch him if you paid me.'

'You used to fancy him girl! You told me you did!' Keesha was insistent.

'Yeah well – whatever. That was before I knew about him.'

But Keesha just laughed. 'You mean like before you realised he's not that into you! And if he not into you girl, then you're right – he's a loser!'

Listening to all of that made me a bit confused. I didn't know what to think. And anyway why did it matter? I'd only seen this Ptolemy bloke once and I might not fancy him at all if I saw him again. Besides, I wasn't going to risk falling out with my new housemates in some pathetic rivalry over a boy. If Mel really fancied him then she was bound to get him – she was the kind of girl any boy would want to be seen with.

'Look, I'm really sorry – I can't come to your party tonight,' I told Keesha and Mel, hurriedly. 'I'd like to come – but it's my little brother. He's gone missing and he like tried to phone me today...' But I didn't need to say any more. Everyone in that room had been in care and there was this kind of bond between us. Keesha put an arm round my shoulder and gave it a squeeze.

Nathan just nodded, those big brown eyes sad and questioning. I suspect he was wondering why I hadn't mentioned it before.

'That's tough,' Mel said, sympathetic now. 'My older sister ran away from our children's home. She came back eventually, but I was that worried about her.'

After that I offered to lend the girls my new vacuum. And they promised to take very good care of it and not to let any losers try to vacuum up glass with it.

'If you change your mind, you jus' come on down,' Keesha told me as she and Mel went out the door, lugging my precious new cleaning machine.

So here I am, writing this diary. I'm also eating a chocolate Hobnob and toasting myself with a cup of tea: 'To Holly Richards and her shiny new future as a brilliant artist.'

SATURDAY 8 AUGUST
Day 3 GIA

I can't quite believe what's been going on! If anyone ever reads this diary they'd say, 'No! It couldn't happen like that!' But it does, it did. Holly Richards is officially in love.

I spent the rest of yesterday afternoon painting. I started to paint some of the trees I can see from this window. They're getting a bit shrivelled in the sun and they look kind of grumpy and sorry for themselves and I want to see if I can get that across in my picture. It's a bit like the sun is at war with the trees and the poor old sky is stuck in between them and doesn't know whose side to be on. I used oranges and reds, but also purples and I wonder what Mrs Wilson would think about my painting. I wonder how she is and whether she's getting used to the idea that her husband is dead. I don't think you ever "get over" someone who isn't around any more, but you just find a way to get used to the fact.

Around 6.30 I started cooking a shepherd's pie with the remains of the food Jane had given me. Nathan went out to basketball practice and came back just after I was grilling the cheesy bit on the top.

'Smells incredible, man,' he said, dumping his sweaty sports kit on the table.

'Shower first!' I said, pointing firmly at the door. 'And put that pongy kit in the laundry basket.' He shrugged and lumbered out of the room. A moment later I heard the click of the laundry basket lid, followed by the lock on the bathroom door. As I brought carrots and baby peas to the boil, I could hear Nathan singing joyfully and tunelessly over the sound of the water.

'You could invite dat blonde girl to Keesh's party,' Nathan suggested hopefully, his mouth full of mashed potato.

'Maybe next time,' I reassured him. I knew that Lucy was seeing the Dreadful Daniel that evening. She'd texted me all excited to say he was taking her to some new club in town. Apparently he knew a bloke who worked on the door, so Lucy would be able to get in without ID.

'So you going then?' I asked Nathan, who shook his head. 'Not my scene,' he replied. But I suspect it would have been if Lucy had agreed to come.

All through supper I wondered what to do about Ryan. Should I phone Donald and tell him about the missed call. Then it occurred to me that maybe the reason Ryan was ringing was to tell me he was back with Kitty and Craig. But surely someone would have told me? In the end I rang Kitty, who answered the phone sounding hopeful as soon as she heard my name. And nearly burst into tears as she admitted that nothing had changed since Sunday.

'I think he tried to call me today,' I blurted out suddenly, wanting to give Kitty some comfort, and instantly regretted it. Maybe she'd suggest we call the police. But instead she suggested that we tell Donald. Donald is superman in Kitty's eyes and can save the planet at a moment's notice.

Donald was transforming in a phone box when I called him. Actually, I think he was saving a kid from a wicked step-parent.

'Holly, so sorry I can't talk just now,' he whispered down the phone. 'We're making a place of safety order on this wee lad...' Donald's voice sounded strange, kind of muffled. 'Oh Holly, you should see the cigarette burns on this little lad's arms... all blistered and going septic. The little lad must be in agony. I'd like to kill the ******* who did this...' Then a moment of silence as Donald pulled his sensible social worker mask back on. 'Sorry about that Holly – that was very unprofessional of me. I should be used to this kind of thing by now, but it gets to me every time. Can I call you back later?'

I said of course he could. A job like Donald's must be tough. It was Friday night and the rest of the world was getting ready to relax and Donald was starting his weekend taking a kid into care. I could just picture him standing around in a street, while a couple of burly policemen bashed down a door – and spoke to the parents. Donald would probably have to go in alongside them and explain to a petrified kid that he must leave the house with him. We've had so many abused kids at Jane and Martin's. Sometimes they talk about their lives, sometimes they don't. But a few of the older ones have told me how they felt when someone finally came to take them out of the nightmare they were living in. Terrified that they were being taken away from the only home and family they knew, and so relieved that the horrible hurt and misery was going to end.

This made me think about little Simon, the new kid. I still didn't know why he was in hospital. I tried to phone Jane and Martin on their landline, but the phone was engaged. I bet they have their hands full with reports and meetings and the usual shindig that starts when a kid in their care gets really ill or hurt or something serious goes wrong. It's a lot of stress for everyone. So I just left a message saying I was thinking of them and I was doing fine – and if it was still alright, I'd come for dinner on Sunday.

I wanted someone to talk to and I knew Lucy would be getting ready for her night out. It wasn't fair to spoil her evening. For a moment I thought of calling Sean but I wasn't sure I was ready to forgive him yet. Although he'd sent me a rather incredible text during the day. It said:

Holly I love you so much, Id do anything 4 u, u know that. But I just feel u take me for grantd. That u got no feelings 4 me. Im not after ur body Hols evn tho its way 2 sexy – I love ur heart and ur mind. And you go on hiding them from me coz u afraid to trust me. Thatz what I think anywayz. And I dn't care if ur x wiv me. Lets talk when u ready to make up. S xxxx

Of course he was wrong about me, but it was good to know he cared so much. But I wasn't quite sure I was ready to talk to him yet. I still hadn't made up my mind whether there was a place for him in my new life.

So I was going to tell everything to this diary, when there was a knock on our front door. I'd heard sounds of snoring coming from the front room and I guessed Nathan had fallen asleep in front of the telly. So shouting 'hang on', I clambered out from under my duvet. I don't know what made me brush my hair but something did. And I was glad I looked so cool in my baby blue pyjamas with the camisole top – as there wasn't time to change into anything else.

'Well look at you!' Mr Green Eyes was standing on the doorstep, grinning and checking me out. 'Like a princess woken from her slumber.'

My heart did a leap, then a backflip. Then a handstand. I knew it was stupid but there was nothing I could do about it. He was leaning against the doorframe, hands dug deep into the pockets of his faded jeans. He was wearing a baggy white shirt with the sleeves rolled up, and that woolly hat I saw last time, pulled down so low it almost covered his eyebrows. And those eyes – they were even greener than I remembered, and all bright and sparkly as he grinned.

'Hello,' I said, hoping I didn't sound as flustered as I felt. 'Are you looking for someone?'

He looked at me for a moment, biting his bottom lip. 'Oh yes,' he said, eventually. 'And I think I may have found her.'

It was like something out of a film, one of those chick flicks. The moment when the really famous actress opens the door and the really famous actor is standing there looking all sheepish and adorable. And they have one of those clever conversations. Except in this case the actor was doing all the clever lines and the actress was wondering when she was going to fluff the script. Because I just couldn't think what to say next.

Fortunately Mr Green Eyes didn't wait for my reply. 'Are you going to ask me in?' he said. And I wanted to say no, because I always play hard to get, but this time I said 'yes'. And before I knew it we were drinking coffee in my bedroom and he was sitting opposite me reading my palm and telling me that something very exciting was just about to happen to me.

I can't remember everything we talked about last night. But we talked for hours and hours and hours. He told me all about growing up between London and Paris – and constantly travelling, with no real place to call home. His mother was a journalist and photographer, and his dad conducted a symphony orchestra. They were always on the move, to wherever his dad was working next, and sometimes (in school holidays) to wherever his mum was sent to cover a story about international terrorists, or about gun runners or gangs or undercover police forces. He'd met street children in Brazil and lost tribes in the Congo. He'd seen a woman shot during a street protest and hundreds of terrified people handcuffed and slung into the back of police vans. He'd been to carnivals that went on for a week and visited prisons where kids lived on the second floor because the ground floor was usually flooded.

He'd spent most of the time in between at a very posh boarding school, which he said he hated, as he hated anything with lots of rules and regulations. But I got the impression that maybe he'd liked it a bit more than he let on – and that sometimes it was the only place that really felt like home. Strange that – in some ways it reminded me of my own life, just a little. Except his parents were choosing to pay for him to live away from them, and the state was paying for me to live with people who were doing their best to make me feel part of their family.

After school he got a place to train to be an actor. It wasn't RADA which I'd heard of but some other place, which Ptolemy said was almost as famous. (He had to tell me how to say his name again; you have to get the end sound right, that long eeee sound has to be there or it sounds like Tol-ee-My which is totally wrong.) He hadn't really known if he wanted to be a movie star or a stage actor, but acting was the only thing he was any good at besides photography – and he didn't really want to be a photographer because that's what his mum did and he wanted to make his own career. But he said that the training started to really irritate him. It was all about digging down inside yourself and analysing your feelings, spending hours in classes learning how the voice works and which bits of the mouth and throat produce different sounds. He found it really boring having to learn huge great chunks of scripts and the people irritated him. Not surprisingly, at the end of the first year they chucked him off the course.

His parents were livid. 'They're such dedicated people,' he explained to me. 'Work is everything. Work is god. It did their heads in that their only son wasn't going to show the same level of commitment to his chosen career. Mum was immediately trying to sign me up for a photography course or get me into another drama school. But I told her I didn't want any of it. I wanted some time just to bum around, to be me and do some of the stuff normal people do. Like get a job in a veggie café and live in a squat with some friends I'd made.'

Part of me was really shocked to hear this. How could anyone with all those advantages be prepared to throw it all away? But I guess the real point was that Tol had never had much say in what happened to him; he'd never had the chance to decide for himself what he really wanted. So here was I feeling sorry for the poor little rich boy – because at least I absolutely totally and one hundred per cent knew what I wanted from life. Which was to be a famous artist, who gets very well paid for her work.

'But my folks just freaked,' Tol continued. 'They said I would soon see that I couldn't live like that. And until I did, they wouldn't give me another penny of their money. If my gran – who is half Russian, half French and lives in Berlin – and is a total sweetheart, although she's pickled in vodka most of the time and smokes like a chimney – didn't send me a cheque every now and again, it would be pretty hard to manage on just my wages. She helped me pay for my new camera – because that's what I'm going to do soon. Become a design and fashion photographer, maybe get into advertising or magazines. My Darling Mother will hate that – she thinks they are sooo shallow.'

Tol still lived in the squat but then he met Saul through a friend of a friend. And Saul let him camp out in the flat upstairs when the squat got too cold, or too hot in the middle of summer. Or the couple who lived in the room next door kept him awake all night with their screaming, drunken rows.

'Cathy found me here a few times but I think she thought I was Saul's boyfriend, and I kind of played along with that. She was trying so hard to show she didn't have any problems with our relationship that she's never questioned how often I stay round here. And now she's hardly ever here and I don't think Phil even knows I exist.'

Saul, he explained, had almost moved out to live with his real boyfriend but he popped in every now and again to have coffee with Phil – which kept everyone happy. And the Bosnian bloke called Stefan stayed in his bedroom most of the time. He was doing a course in economics and studied round the clock, and was a bit of a recluse. 'So the flat's sort of become my second home,' Tol told me, grinning in that way that made my heart do press-ups round the edges.

I wondered what the tax-payers would think about this situation. It would make a nice story if one of the local papers got hold of it. Flats for kids leaving care become refuge for dossing toff. But that was a bit unkind really. Tol had his own problems and Phil and Cathy were doing their best. They couldn't know what's going down here 24 hours a day or it would be some kind of prison.

While we talked the music from downstairs was getting louder and louder, but I didn't really mind. It was summer time and people were entitled to party if they wanted to. Tol asked if I wanted to go and join them and I said yes, just for a little while. So he sat in the kitchen while I put on my strappy little black dress and my new red boots. Tol did a mock faint when I appeared. And he kissed me then, for the first time. The room spun round, I swear it.

We went into the party holding hands but everyone was so busy drinking, dancing and having a good time that nobody noticed us. Until I saw Mel talking with some girls by the window. I was dancing with Ptolemy with my head resting on his shoulder and I caught her eye. She gave me this really quizzical look, then seemed to think better of it and looked away. I didn't know what to make of that.

Keesha was at the centre of everything, boogying her gorgeous legs off. She was even more amazing than before, dressed in a mauve spangly catsuit that clung to her curvy body like a glove. She had long, straight black hair this time but with a big silver lightning flash sprayed into it. Guys were circling around her like flies at the honey pot, but her eyes were closed and she was giving it all to the music. That girl will be someone really famous one day, I'm sure of it.

Sometime round 3am we got tired of dancing – and anyway I couldn't wait any longer. Tol's body against mine felt so good and I wanted to get as close to him as I could, so there were no barriers between us. We slipped away and went to my room.

Some people say the first time is a big disappointment but it wasn't like that for me. OK, so the first time isn't all lights and bells and whistles, and to be honest I was a bit scared and a bit excited, but most of all nervous about making sure the right bits went in the right places and I didn't do anything stupid. And that it didn't hurt too much. But Tol was patient and gentle and it was much better than I expected.

But when we did it for the second time it was brilliant – and totally different. It was like something caught fire inside me and these red and orange flames started creeping up through my body until I was one big burning bonfire. And nothing mattered except my body and Tol's, and it was wild and beautiful, and selfish and shared – all at the same time. And when I collapsed on Tol's chest and he stroked my hair and murmured my name, over and over again, it was like a little bit of heaven on earth. And I wanted to hold on to that moment for ever, because I knew it was precious and special for me. And I knew then I'd been right to wait until the perfect person came along.

I woke up shortly after eight o'clock with Tol flat on his back and snoring gently beside me. Even when he snores he's the most beautiful man in the world. I curled up with my head on his shoulder and he stirred in his sleep and wriggled an arm around me. I lay listening to the sound of his heart until I fell asleep again.

Tol had gone when I woke up. He left me a note which said: *Gorgeous Girl I have stuff to do. See ya tonite. Call ya later.* And then this PS saying *I love you Lady in the Red Shoes*.

And the weird thing is that I know he means it. And I know also that I love him too. So I've made myself scrambled egg on toast and a great big pot of tea – which is nearly cold now, and I've written it all down. I don't think I've ever been so happy in my life and I don't want to forget about any of it.

SUNDAY 9 AUGUST
Day 4 GIA

I was looking forward to seeing my foster family today but I think they understood when I said something really important had come up. Tol said it was the perfect day to go to Cambridge and I knew he was right. I'd never been to Cambridge before but he lived there for a while when he was a kid. He told me all about how you could go punting down the river. I've seen it in those films, where the woman wears a floaty dress and sits at the front of the punt trailing her hands in the water. And the man stands up at the back of the boat, looking all romantic and noble, and uses a long pole to push the boat along. And then they stop somewhere by a shady bank and they eat a perfect picnic and sip champagne from posh glasses. And she says, 'Nigel, this is splendid,' and he says 'Camilla, I adore you,' and he reads her poetry and she lies back on the picnic rug and looks at the sky and wonders how far away the sun is.

And it was kind of like that, except my boyfriend wasn't that good at punting but I was, so we took it in turns. And we hadn't got a picnic or champagne, just some sandwiches and Kitkats and a bottle of Diet Pepsi we'd bought from a shop near the train station.

But Tol did read a poem he said he'd written just for me, and it was amazing. But then he confessed it wasn't really his, just something he'd found in a book and *wished* he'd written for me. And he'd brought his camera along and took loads of pictures of the water and all the grand buildings in the background, and all the people out on the river having a laugh and lapping up the sunshine. And quite a lot of me – and I was smiling in every one of them, like someone who just won the Lottery.

And we made love in the long grass when there was no one around, just some cows staring at us and chewing the grass and making those low, mooing sounds. I felt a bit embarrassed at first but Tol said that what we were doing was very natural and cows like things that are natural. And I decided he was right, because it did feel like the most natural thing I'd ever done. And after we'd done it once, we did it again. But then we realised it was getting late and we'd get charged extra if we didn't get the punt back on time.

After we took the punt back, we wandered around and looked at some of the colleges. They're so amazing – some of them are hundreds of years old, with great big areas of grass and their own chapels and libraries. Tol told me that the colleges at Cambridge are different to the college that I'm going to. They're all part of the University of Cambridge but each college is different. So they have maybe 200 students living in the college, who sleep there and eat there and hang out there and maybe have a gym and a common room and TV and pool table there, and they also have their own tutor in the college. But during the day, they go to other parts of Cambridge for lectures, to study with people from other colleges. So you get to meet loads of different people, and some of them have travelled from the other side of the world. Although today there weren't many students around because it's summer holidays, just Japanese tourists going 'ooh' and 'aah' (or whatever the expression is in Japanese) and taking photographs of all the grand buildings and the spires and rooftops of the town.

I said I thought it would be really cool to be a student in Cambridge. I could fancy having one of those bedrooms with the really old-fashioned windows – like something from a castle or stately home – and look out onto all the green spaces and walkways, and all those other students wheeling their bikes and chatting about what they'd learned that day and which pub they were going to later. And I started wondering if they did any kind of art courses or whether I might decide to study something like philosophy or English. Just so I could come here.

But Tol said it reminded him of being at boarding school and he wouldn't like it at all. But I don't see it like that. I think it would be good to have your own little space in the middle of all this grandness, knowing that you were just one of thousands of students who'd lived in your college since it was built.

I didn't want to leave Cambridge but Tol said he needed to do something in the evening so we had to get back. I hoped he was going to ask me along as well but I don't want to turn into one of those clingy girlfriends who has to be with her man all the time.

It's not that I mind being on my own this evening, it's just it would have been good if someone was around. And I really wanted to see Lucy and tell her about my wonderful boyfriend called Ptolemy, but she was out with Mr Wrong. And nobody else seemed to be around in the house. Nathan was out and I did wonder about whether it would be OK to knock on Mel and Keesha's door, but there was absolute silence from their flat so I guessed they were either out or fast asleep.

So I rang Jane who sounded a bit hassled, but she said it was because she was so worried about Simon. He's been swallowing things again – which is apparently why he got taken to hospital last time. Jane thought he might have swallowed some paperclips, but she wasn't really sure. He seemed alright and she thought it might be better to wait until morning to take him to the hospital for a check-up.

Jane asked what Donald had said and I realised then that Donald had never called me back. Even worse, I realised that I hadn't thought about my little brother for nearly two days. It wasn't that I'd exactly forgotten about him, I'd just let him slip to the back of my mind because there was so much other stuff going on.

I told Jane about Tol – but not everything. I said I'd met a really nice lad through the new place and I was very keen on him. Jane said that was good and asked if I had finished with Sean, and then I felt a bit guilty because I'd never replied to Sean's last text.

After Jane hung up I started writing a Dear John email to Sean. One of the girls from school got dumped by her boyf on Facebook and she cried for days and days. I thought that was so mean and I'd made a promise that I'd always tell Sean properly when it was over. But Tol rang while I was doing it and told me how much he loved me and how he couldn't wait to see me tomorrow. That made me feel brilliant but also a bit sad for Sean. I didn't mention anything in the email about Tol – just said I needed a bit of space and I didn't feel about him like he felt about me. And that I hoped we could still be friends. I'm sure he'll get another girlfriend sometime. He's the kind of guy that girls are always noticing, but I know he's very fussy.

I'm going to text Ryan and ask him to contact me, and tomorrow I'll call Donald and tell him about the missed phone call. Then I'm going to have an early night and watch TV in bed.

MONDAY 10 AUGUST
Day 6 of GIA

Today was probably the most perfect day ever. Ptolemy rang me early – and said I was missing a fantastic sunrise, so of course I had to get up and take a look. He was right, it was an awesome morning. He said I should try and paint it. So I did. But I put lots of my feelings for him into the painting as well – so there's colours in there like turquoise and magenta because those are the colours he makes me feel.

Tol didn't have to work today, so we met in town and took a bus to one of those villages that lies to the west of Corrington. It's a pretty place with lots of old-worldy houses, some of them with thatched roofs. There's a duck pond and a cricket pitch and a little village shop that sells eggs and milk from a local farm, and the window is full of posters drawn by little kids advertising their school play and the village fête and a bring-and-buy sale – all faded in the heat and curling round the edges. Most of them happened like months ago but nobody has remembered to take them down.

My boyfriend wanted to go to a pub which he said brewed its own ale. I hate beer of any sorts and it tasted like drinking warm cat's pee to me. I told Tol this and he said how did I know, had I ever drunk cat's pee, and I had to admit that it was only a guess. But I had a non-alcoholic summer fruit cocktail, which the barman made for me specially, and we ordered chicken which came with these homemade chips that were big and chunky – all soft in the middle but really crisp on the outside. I think they were the most delicious chips I've ever eaten.

After we'd eaten we went for a walk round the village. Tol bought me ice cream from an ice-cream van, and he did silly impersonations of the voices he thought sheep would have if they could speak. And he kissed me lots of times under the trees and it was so romantic I thought we were in a rom-com or something.

Later we went back to Corrington and I checked my email and there was a message from Sean saying he'd got my email and didn't know what to say. He tried to make some jokey comment about how if he was a knight he'd probably fall on his sword, but I could tell he was upset. I felt mean but it couldn't be helped. I wasn't going to let it spoil my day. I rang Donald again but he was still on voicemail. Maybe he's having a day off – but I don't believe in miracles.

I left Nathan a note to say there was some shop-bought cheese and broccoli flan in the fridge and he could heat it up with a can of beans. I'm sure even he can manage that. And I reminded him to put his kit in the wash when he gets in from football. (I've made him write on the calendar when he's going to be out late coz I don't want to be cooking stuff if he's not around.)

Tol took me to see this band that he said I would like. They were OK but not the kind of music I'd listen to ordinarily. But somehow with Tol everything is better than normal. The pub was small and cramped and the music was much too loud to hear yourself think, but Tol was full of energy and chatted away to me all the time. And I was dead happy, just sitting there beside him and holding his hand, and watching those beautiful green eyes as they darted all over the room.

We spent part of the night in Tol's room – it's a bit of a tip and all Saul's stuff is still stacked in boxes round the edges, but it's in the attic and the window opens really wide, so it's cooler than mine. He was dead passionate and it was probably like the best time ever. But afterwards neither of us could sleep. Sometimes it's so intense being near Tol that I feel like my insides are being wound round a stick or something. So I came down to my room and I'm writing this. I think if you can write things down, then you stop going over and over them in your mind. Then I'll see if I can sleep.

TUESDAY 11 AUGUST
Day 7 GIA

It was good that Tol had to work today coz I had washing to do and some tidying up around the flat. With Nathan and Ptolemy leaving mess all weekend it looked like a bomb had hit it. I was in the laundry room, trying to force the powder drawer to close when Mel came in. She was wearing a dressing gown and her hair was all messed up and standing on end. She had streaks of last night's mascara down her cheeks. But she still managed to look pretty cool.

'Thanks for the party,' I said as she unloaded a heap of clothes into one of the machines. She nodded and yawned, and rubbed her eyes vigorously with the back of her hand.

'You with that Tol'mee guy now, then?' she asked, trying to sound like it didn't mean anything.

'Sort of – I mean, it's just a casual thing,' I said, unsure why I felt it so important to keep my true feelings from Mel. 'I have a boyfriend – from before I moved here,' I said suddenly. I have no idea why I told her this.

'You should stick with him then,' Mel said, fixing me with her panda-rimmed eyes.

I hate it when people tell me what to do, especially people who hardly know me. But I quite like Mel and I didn't want to fall out with my new neighbours. 'Why's that?' I asked, guardedly.

'That guy's got issues.'

Who doesn't have, I thought. Turned out by his family and living on other people's floors, you couldn't exactly expect Tol to be problem free. 'Sure. I know about them,' I said quickly, feeling protective towards the person I love.

'Well so long as you do...' Mel was lighting a cigarette. 'Not that it's any of my business of course...I mean he's a nice enough guy and everything...'

And she was right – it wasn't any of her business. And I couldn't help feel that Mel was just a bit jealous that I'd got Tol when she hadn't. Although I'm not sure he'd really be her type. I think she's quite a tough cookie, not the kind to go for men who are sensitive or need a bit of emotional support.

Keesha came in just then, all bouncy and full of life and wearing a very short nightshirt with stars and stripes all over it. Her hair was up in a towel and she was already in a fresh layer of make up. She was full of news about the party she'd been to the night before and some famous DJ who had given her his number and told her to call him "anytime". I had to pretend I knew who she was talking about.

Keesha wanted me to go shopping with them but I said I had things to do. I knew I had to try Donald again.

Donald picked up on my second ring. He sounded dead guilty to hear my voice. I knew he'd completely forgotten that he was supposed to be calling me back. But you know what? It kind of endeared him to me. That man is always such a saint, it's nice to know he gets stuff wrong sometimes.

Donald said that there was no news about Ryan. The police were treating him as a missing person case but they didn't seem to be taking it very seriously. He'd gone missing too many times before.

'But never this long! Never for over a week!' I blurted out.

'They say that it's probably just a sign that he's getting older,' Donald tried to reassure me. 'They seem pretty confident that he'll turn up any day now.'

'In other words they're not even bothering!' I felt so angry that my little brother wasn't that important. If he was some small child with blonde curls and a cute smile they'd probably have half the country out searching for him.

I told Donald about the missed call and he said it was a really good sign. He promised to ring the police and pass on the information. I said I was happy to give a statement. I'll do anything to get my little brother back.

WEDNESDAY 12 AUGUST
Day 8 GIA

Today was a weird kind of day. It started with me being woken up by Tol falling onto the bed. He then started to laugh about something he'd seen out of the window which he thought was very funny, but I didn't get it at all. I asked him how he got in and he said, 'with a key of course,' and I asked what key and he said, 'a key to the door'. Which he seemed to think was even funnier and he got a fit of giggles and couldn't stop. I asked him if he was drunk and he said maybe, and I said I didn't like it when people were drunk and he said, 'I can go and sleep upstairs if you want.' And I think he meant it, so I said no, it was OK if he stayed with me. Because by now I was starting to feel quite awake and I'd remembered just how good it feels to have Tol's warm body beside me.

But when he got into bed he didn't seem to want to hold me at all. 'I'm tired', he said and rolled over and fell asleep. Just like that. I lay awake for ages feeling really cross with him and a bit hurt that he could treat me that way. And when I did fall asleep I had one of my nightmares about Ryan. I woke up shaking and sweating but my boyfriend didn't seem to notice. In the end I shook him and he eventually woke up. He took me in his arms then and kissed me until I felt a lot better.

In the morning, Tol was kind of edgy. He said he'd had a bad night too and needed some fresh air. I said we could go for a walk, but he told me he was going to have a smoke and he knew I hated that, so he'd see me later. I said that was fine because I had plans for the day and I would probably be busy this evening. But Tol just told me he loved me and said he'd see me at supper time. He really doesn't listen sometimes that boy, I think it's maybe that he learned to switch off when he was at boarding school.

I rang Jane to tell her that I'd managed to speak to Donald. I felt a bit irritated because I could tell Jane had other things on her mind. I move out one week and the next it's like she's forgotten all about me. Then she said something that really shook me.

'Tell me that again,' I said to Jane, because to be honest I hadn't been listening properly. 'What did you just say about Lucy?'

Jane let out a big sigh – like she had all the cares of the world on her shoulder and maybe she has. She takes on too much sometimes, that woman. 'It's not that I'm absolutely sure or anything,' she told me confidentially, 'but Lucy is being sick an awful lot. She thinks I don't know about it but she can't seem to hold food down for any time at all. I've asked her if she's feeling alright but she just smiles and says it's a bit of a stomach bug – all the summer fruit or something like that. Then I think that maybe I'm just being paranoid. But if you could talk to her Holly, I think she would tell you – because if she is pregnant then she has to face up to the reality. And that isn't Lucy's strong point – as we both know.'

OMG! It's finally come to this. I've been kind of worrying about it for several weeks now but trying to tell myself that Lucy was OK. I told Jane that I would talk to Lucy as soon as I could. I think Jane was hoping I'd say that she was just imagining it and there was no way that Lucy was in trouble, but I couldn't see any point lying to her.

'And try to come for supper on Sunday, Holly, it isn't the same without you here. We're all missing you,' Jane said, just before she put down the phone. 'Bring that young man you were talking about – if you want to, of course.'

I've texted Lucy to ask her when she's free to meet up. And I've tried Ryan again but there's still no answer. But now I have to get myself dressed up, coz Tol just rang to say we're going to the movies tonight. The film sounds a bit naff but I don't really care. Sitting beside him in the dark when he does that thing, where he lifts my hand and softly kisses the inside of my wrists, which sends little currents of electricity all over my body – that's enough for me.

THURSDAY 13 AUGUST
Day 9 GIA

Lucy agreed to meet me at the swimming pool. She was keen to get Mr Giraffe back and even keener, she said, to see me. Lucy swims like a fish and she's never happier than when she's in the water. She was on the county team for a bit when she was younger, and I used to go to the pool with her on cold winter mornings, just so she had a bit of company. Today it was totally tropical in the pool. It was almost as hot inside as it was out, and there were kids and adults jumping about and splashing, and steaming the air up even more with all that moving around. The lifeguard looked half asleep. Or maybe he'd just given up telling people not to run, dive, bomb, snog or whatever it is that you're forbidden from doing by those black and white signs with the big Xs across them. He did wake up a bit when he saw Lucy in her blue and pink bathing cozzie, with her blonde curls swept up into a ponytail. Lucy has that effect on men. Lucy likes her food and she doesn't care who knows it. In the pictures I've seen of her as a baby, she was one of those chubby kids with dimpled knees and podgy little hands. She looked adorable then, and these days – as a curvy size 14 – she looks just as adorable now.

We swam thirty lengths and avoided a gang of adolescent boys who kept trying alternatively to dive bomb us and chat us up. After we'd swum we sat on the edge of the pool and I decided it was time for the "difficult conversation".

'Your mum is dead worried about you,' I said, because I just couldn't think of any other way to start it.

Lucy just smiled her happy-go-lucky smile and said, 'Mum's always worrying about something. You know that.'

'Yeah, but this time she's really worried – I mean she's not sure if you're OK. If there's something really wrong, if you're like...' I couldn't bring myself to use the word "pregnant". Not with a gaggle of toddlers and their mothers bobbing up and down in the water next to us.

'Well, me and Daniel are finished now. Mum doesn't need to worry any more,' Lucy told me calmly.

'Finished?' I couldn't keep the surprise out of my voice. 'When did that happen?'

'The other night, at the club, he was behaving like a total prat. Showing off and flashing his money around and flirting with the waitresses. I was that embarrassed to be seen with him. Then this woman comes over, she was old enough to be his gran, and he was all over her...it just grossed me out.'

'What, in front of you?'

'Yeah, right in front of me. Like I wasn't there or something.' Lucy tossed her head and got hit in the eye by the wet end of the ponytail. You could see it hurt a bit but she just burst out laughing. This was the old Lucy, the Lucy I'd grown up with.

'And you know what?' she continued. 'As I watched him, I suddenly saw what a pathetic little jerk he is. He's not even that fit. I can't really see what I saw in him...So I said I was going to the Ladies. But I didn't. I left the club and rang Dad to come and pick me up. I told him I'd had a row with my mate and wasn't staying over at her house after her "party". I told him I'd be waiting in the bus shelter and he just came and got me. No questions asked.'

'That's coz he trusts you,' I said, watching Lucy's cheeks going very pink.

Lucy told me that Daniel had been trying to contact her ever since. He'd even sent her a giant pink rabbit clutching a box of chocolates. 'It isn't the bunny's fault, so I'm keeping him – but I gave the chocolates to the little kids. They were a bit melted. But it's just so over with me and that freak,' Lucy assured me. 'I never want to see his pathetic face again.'

This was good news but it wasn't answering the big question about was she or wasn't she. 'So are you OK? I mean is everything OK now?'

Lucy laughed 'Stop fussing Hols. I'm not going to die of a broken heart if that's what's bothering you.'

I had to get to the point. I edged closer to Lucy and whispered into her ear. 'Your Mum thinks you're pregnant? You aren't, are you?'

Lucy knotted her forehead. 'Mum is such an idiot sometimes. Why didn't she just come right out and ask me? If she's that worried.'

'She says she has asked you. That you just say you've got a tummy bug or something. She says you've been sick after every meal.'

'That's stupid...' But Lucy looked more uncomfortable now. I wasn't going to let this rest.

'So if you aren't pregnant Luce, then why all the throwing up?'

My foster sister just shook her head. 'Mum is exaggerating. You know what she's like.'

But Jane isn't someone who fusses. She's seen far too many situations where kids have real problems and she doesn't make mountains out of molehills.

Then in a flash it all clicked into place. 'Luce – you're not making yourself throw up, are you? You're not getting bulimic or something?'

'Of course not! Can you honestly imagine me going off my food?' Lucy said hurriedly. 'Let's swim again; it's hot sitting here.'

After we left the pool I suggested to Lucy that we went to that new place that does milkshakes and smoothies. She always loves it and usually has a milkshake and a smoothie, because she can never decide which one she likes most. But today she didn't want to go. 'It's too hot for that. Let's go for a walk in the park,' she said. 'We can get something to drink there. They've got a café by the pond.'

Swimming always makes me starving hungry and I was ready for a great big slice of the death-by-chocolate cake they had in the café. With a full-fat can of Coke. But Lucy said she only wanted a Diet Pepsi. But as I ate my cake I could see Lucy watching every mouthful, like some lion watching a gazelle and wondering when to pounce. 'You want a bit?' I asked her, but she shook her head.

I was still hungry after the cake so I went to get something else. 'Can I just have a little bit of that?' Lucy said eyeing up my cheese and tomato sandwich. I gave her half of it but she took it and tore a bit off the corner, and gave most of it back to me. She nibbled it carefully for a minute and then made a big point of looking at the ducks. But almost straight away she reached out and tore off another little bit from my plate and stuffed it quickly into her mouth. And that way Lucy ate most of my sandwich – bit by bit.

'I've got something to tell you,' I said, as soon as I'd finished stuffing my own face. But I could tell Lucy wasn't really listening. 'I need to go to the toilet,' she said, 'I'll be back in a min...'

'Sit down and listen first to what I have to tell you. You're never going to believe this Luce.'

'OK, but I really do need to go. I might wet myself or something...'

I didn't believe her for a minute, but what could I do? 'Fine – but be quick. I have some awesome news to tell you.'

Lucy was gone for more than five minutes. I timed her. Her eyes had that slightly bloodshot look you get when you've just heaved your guts up. 'I just stuck my mascara brush in my eye – it stung something wicked,' she told me. But I was pretty sure she was lying.

She was all ready then to hear about my big news. And she almost fell off the chair when I told her about the night of the Red Boots.

'Well, I hope you took precautions – otherwise Mum will be worrying about you too!'

I told her that of course I took precautions. Tol was the kind of person who always had something with him "just in case". 'Not that he's a slag or anything,' I told Lucy quickly. 'He's just very thoughtful and considerate.' But Lucy laughed loudest of all when I told her I was in love. 'I don't believe you!' she thumped the table, to make her point. 'You don't do love, Hols. You've never done love!'

'Maybe that's coz I never met the right bloke before,' I told her, sounding like some dippy heroine in a chick flick.

Lucy told me she couldn't wait to meet him and I told her that Jane had suggested I bring him to supper on Sunday. Lucy said that was really cool and I said I couldn't guarantee anything because Tol was a busy guy and couldn't always be pinned down. But I made a mental note that I'd go round to the house on Sunday anyway. I'd have to talk to Jane about Lucy's eating disorder.

We hung out until almost dark and then I went back to my new flat. Nathan was eating chips out of paper in the kitchen and looked quite peeved when I came in. 'Oops sorry,' I said. 'I should have been home to cook supper.'

'That Torolee bloke – he's waitin' for you, in your room,' Nathan nodded towards the door, glaring. 'He used up all the milk.'

That was rich coming from Nathan who never had anything in the fridge till I moved in. 'Did you find the shopping list I left for you?' I asked him curtly. 'There was fresh milk on that list. And I left you ten pounds towards my half of it.'

Nathan shook his head. 'I didn't see no list.'

'What's that?' I pointed at an envelope in the middle of the table. It had Nathan's name written clearly on the front of it. 'I know you can read coz you've got all those textbooks on sports physio and stuff. Or do you just look at the pictures?' (I didn't mean to sound so sarcastic, but I was tired and it had been a long, hot day.)

Nathan glared at me. 'I thought dat was a note from Keesh. She leaves me notes when she wants to borrow money.'

I didn't bother asking why he wasn't capable of telling his own sister's handwriting from mine. I just wanted to get out of the kitchen and see Tol.

My lovely man was fast asleep on my bed when I found him. One hand slung casually on the pillows above his head. The other curled tightly over his heart. On his face was the most wonderful smile, as innocent and untroubled as a newborn baby. I stroked his cheek but he just fluttered his long eyelashes and continued to sleep as deeply as before. I kissed his mouth very gently, and then left him.

I can hear his deep, contented breathing as I write this journal.

FRIDAY 14 AUGUST
Day 10 GIA

Today is Ryan's 14th birthday. I'm trying not to think about it too much or I'll get really upset. But I hope wherever he is – he knows that I'm thinking about him.

I asked Ptolemy this morning what time he started work in the café and he looked surprised. He said he hadn't worked there for several months. That he'd lost his job after an argument with the owner, who refused to let staff have any of the tips that customers left them. I couldn't blame him for leaving because of that, but it made me feel a bit uneasy not knowing how Tol was making his money. And although he wasn't exactly flush, he wasn't short either.

But my boyf can read me like a book. 'So now you're wondering how I make my living,' he said smiling. 'Am I a burglar or a drug dealer? Is it the big car and all the bling that gives me away?' Which made me laugh. Tol doesn't wear any sort of jewellery at all, not even a ring or one of those leather-thong pendants which some of the Emo boys wear.

'Actually I've been doing some photography, if you really want to know,' he told me very casually.

'Photography?' I said. 'What kind of photography?' Please don't let it be something sleazy, I prayed. I didn't want a boyfriend exploiting women who have to take their clothes off to pay their rent or feed their children.

'For an agency,' he replied, a little warily.

'What kind of agency?' I asked, way too eagerly.

Tol shrugged. 'We artists have to eat, my princess,' he said, but there was a teasing look in his eyes.

'Actually it's a private detective agency,' he told me after a moment. 'It's hardly Fleet Street, but it brings in enough to live on.'

'You mean following people whose partners suspect them of having an affair? Trying to catch them in compromising positions or whatever?'

'Sadly nothing quite as glamorous as that.' Tol gave me a small smile and my heart did some triple backflips. (It should be getting used to those smiles by now. If this goes on much longer I'm going to enter it for the Olympics.) 'It's petty insurance stuff and things like that...people who say that an accident has left them unable to work but they're actually working on a building site six days a week. While their ex-employer is having to pay out thousands in compensation. I get to sit on a lot of benches and sometimes my boss lends me his car. It's not work I'm exactly proud of...'

'Which is why you let me believe you were still working in the café?'

'I didn't actually say I was still working there...' Tol hung his head in that charming boyish way, which even a saint couldn't resist. How could you stay cross with someone that cute?

'Yeah, but you didn't exactly say you weren't. And you've not mentioned the photo work before. Honesty is dead important to me, Tol. I thought you knew that.'

'And I thought that maybe if I told you too early on you'd be disappointed and not want to be with me, so I let you believe I was working in a sweaty veggie kitchen, peeling onions and crying into the soup, while I took artistic and fascinating pictures of rats and dustbins during my coffee breaks. But I wanted to save up some money for rent. I don't like having to rely on other people, even when they're as gorgeous as you, Hollyberry.'

That made me feel all warm inside and of course I forgave him straight away. 'Don't lie to me about anything again – or cover anything up, which is really the same as lying,' I told him, meaning it but not wanting to sound too stern.

'I won't – I don't. There is nothing else you need to know about me,' Tol said and wrapped his arms around me. He kissed my eyelids and I listened to our hearts beating for a bit, and then he started to kiss my neck and it sent little shivers down my spine and my whole body went kind of tingly. I rested my head on his chest and thought it would be nice to die in that moment – because it was so perfect.

Tol left for work and I had some studying I wanted to do. I've ordered most of my course books over the internet and I'm determined to get as much reading as possible done before the term starts. Reading about art isn't as good as doing art, but it's still interesting to find out how other painters see things and the approaches they take to their work.

Sean texted me this morning. He hasn't been in touch for a few days and I admit I've been avoiding him. His text was chatty – just a 'how are you? What's going on with you? Hope we can still be friends' kind of text. There was an air of resignation about it, like he'd accepted that we were no longer an item. I decided to leave it a day or two before I text back, for his sake.

At midday I was having a sandwich in the kitchen when Nathan appeared, laden down with shopping bags. I helped him unload them and then made him a cup of coffee. As we were drinking it, he said, 'You and that Whatsit goin' out together then?'

I said yes, we were seeing quite a lot of each other. Nathan said he realised this, because 'Whatsit' was around so often.

'D'you have a problem with that?' I asked.

Nathan shook his head but then said, 'Yeah, I suppose I do. Just coz he's always here and I thought it was like supposed to be you and me in dis place.'

My first reaction was anger. I'd already brought so much order to the flat – it was clean, tidy and the cupboards were now properly stocked. And the bathroom was so clean you could eat your dinner off the floor (although that wouldn't be a good idea as you'd probably get poisoned by the chemicals in the cleaners). If I wanted to have my boyfriend round, surely Nathan has no reason to moan? But then I remembered something. How annoyed I felt when we'd just seen a foster child leave and it looked like it was just Jane, Martin, Lucy and me in the house for a week or two. Before the next ones moved in. Then I'd come home from school and there'd be a moody adolescent slumped in front of the TV and hogging the remote control. And Jane mouthing 'emergency placement' at me, as she passed me in the hall.

'You should have said something,' I replied rather grumpily.

'I just did.'

I could see it was a big effort for Nathan to hold his ground. He's a very easygoing person and he'd clearly had to think about how to tell me this. But I couldn't pretend I wasn't ruffled. It's not like Nathan doesn't have a million and one really irritating habits that I'm having to live with. 'OK, OK,' I said. 'I get your point. Tol and I will have to spend time together in the upstairs flat. It's cooler up there, even if it's like a real tip.'

Nathan knitted his big shaggy eyebrows. 'You don't need to do dat Holly...it's just like...I mean...' he was then lost for words. But I left the kitchen in a huff, slamming the door behind me.

I went back to my room and pretended to continue reading

but I couldn't concentrate. I wasn't sure if I was really angry with Nathan or just angry with myself for getting into a situation where someone had the upper hand over me. It's not something I'm used to. At Jane and Martin's I'm usually the one explaining to younger kids when they're over-stepping the line.

I heard Nathan go out somewhere round three o'clock. With the coast clear I went back into the kitchen – I was gasping for a cold drink. It gets hot in my room during the afternoons, because the safety lock prevents the window from opening fully. I'll have to buy a fan if this scorching weather continues. I was just making myself some iced coffee when there was a knock at the front door. Tol, I thought, although it was earlier than I was expecting him.

A woman with curly blonde hair, and wearing one of those voluminous patchwork kaftan things that I thought you only saw in fashion exhibitions about the 1960s, was standing outside. Smiling so much it seemed her moon-shaped face would fill the doorway, she held out a clammy hand. 'I'm Cathy,' she said. 'You must be Holly.' She reminded me of one of those children's TV programme types – the big jolly, badly dressed ones that play someone's eccentric aunty. They always live on a barge or in a cottage near a wood – and the main character goes to hide out with them when the aliens take over the school, or MI5 is tracking them down for discovering the secret password.

'I'm soooooo sorry I haven't been round before, but Phil tells me you've settled in splendidly.' She stepped over the threshold without me inviting her in. I could do nothing but follow her to the kitchen and offer to make her some iced coffee.

'I really shouldn't – all those calories,' she bit her lip. 'But I suppose if you've got semi-skimmed milk and you don't add any sugar,' my visitor said, making herself at home on one of the stools. 'I honestly think I shall melt if the weather goes on like this. You pretty young girls in your flimsy little summer frocks – it makes me that envious I could throttle you.' And saying this she laughed a great big, hearty laugh that ended abruptly in a snort.

'Nathan's a sweetie, isn't he? Such a good thing you moved in here. He's a quiet boy and as much as he and Keesh simply adore each other, they were really getting on each other's nerves,' Cathy confided in me, in a low voice.

'It's OK. Nathan is out,' I said. 'Was there anything in particular you wanted to talk to me about?'

Cathy looked taken aback by my question. 'Er no, nothing in particular. This is what you might call a social call, just to see how you're doing. But I can see already that you're doing just fine... I've never seen one of these flats look so clean. Quite, quite amazing. Phil said you were a remarkable young woman.'

I knew there was something more to come, something she hadn't said yet. But I wasn't in the mood to help her out. So I just sipped my cold coffee and waited for her to continue.

Cathy rambled on for a bit, telling me about her job. How she tried to be at the flats as much as possible but couldn't be here as much as she'd like to be. But that didn't mean she didn't care and I must always feel I could call her any time I wanted to, although preferably not at two o'clock in the morning. Although she didn't really mind that either. Honestly she didn't. Did I have her mobile number?

I assured her that Phil had given me a whole list of numbers to call if there was a problem. I'd spoken to him a few times as I passed his office on the way out, and each time I saw him he thrust another list of some kind into my hand (bus maps of the area, free sporting facilities, details of local banks and supermarkets, where to go for debt help and information about nutrition and budgeting). 'But there haven't been any problems and I don't really imagine there are going to be any,' I told Cathy in what I hoped was a very reassuring kind of voice. I really wanted to get rid of her now.

She was nice enough but I had better things to do than sit in the kitchen and make idle chitchat.

'Yes, yes. Of course. I mean why would there be? As I say, Phil says you're very capable. Very capable indeed, except – and don't take this the wrong way – he is a bit concerned about something…'

Just what I needed, another person who wanted to moan at me. 'He hasn't said anything to me,' I told her. Hoping my face didn't look as angry as I felt. I hate it when people beat around the bush; if there's a problem they should tell me, not get someone else to do their dirty work.

'Phil would have said something himself but he thought it was better if I spoke to you – he knows he's not always the most tactful of people. And it's not a real problem, just something he's noticed and is a bit concerned about.'

What is it with these people and their "not a big problem". If it's not a big problem then just spit it out. 'So what is this "concern" then?' I asked, feeling my voice getting icy.

'Oh, it's nothing you've done wrong, dear – nothing like that at all.' Cathy reached across and patted me on the arm. 'I wouldn't want you to think that, no indeed. It's just he's – well, we're a bit worried about someone you seem to be spending time with, who might not be the right kind of company for a girl like you.' (She spoke the words "girl like you" as if the letters were spelt out in cut-glass crystal.)

'Honestly, I'm tougher than you think. I can look after myself,' I said, looking Cathy full in the eyes but a bit puzzled by who this person was she was about to warn me against. Was it Mel and Keesh? Did she think one of them was going to lead me astray with all their wild partying?

'Of course dear, we know you're a very sensible girl. But it's just that you might not have come across people like him before…'

Ah, so this was going to be a lecture about Tol. What had that weasel Nathan been saying to Phil? Or was it Mel and her sour grapes?

'We've – I mean Phil – has seen you a few times with that friend of Saul's. I believe he's Saul's boyfriend...' she said in a rush, going even pinker in the face than she already was. 'And Phil heard a rumour – I don't know where from – that this guy is a drug dealer or something. Of course, it might not be true. He says Saul denies it totally but of course Saul would...and Saul's a bit older than you dear, and I think he's probably used to handling these things.' (The old stereotypes from the telly about all gay men being into drugs and clubs and dancing till dawn...I had actually met Saul's boyfriend on the stairs the other day – with Saul. Saul was a pretty serious-looking kind of guy who Tol had told me wanted to be a marine engineer. And his boyfriend was a shy, rather handsome man in his mid-20s, who Saul introduced as a lecturer in economics at the university.)

I couldn't help but laugh. 'That's just ridiculous,' I said, picturing the fresh-faced man in the open-necked shirt with the sleeves rolled up, wearing sensible lace-up shoes. 'Saul's boyfriend's a university lecturer, and as far as I know he's squeaky clean. I'd imagine it was more than his job was worth. But anyway, are you sure you have the right person? Are you sure this person is Saul's boyfriend?'

Cathy looked totally confounded. I felt a tiny bit guilty because I knew I was deliberately misleading her, but it served her right for listening to stupid rumours.

'Er – to be honest, dear I can't be totally sure. Not having been around myself, and only hearing it from Phil, who really cares about you, and everyone else who lives here of course. It's not that he doesn't trust you, it was just that he was a bit worried and...' but Cathy visibly sagged, like a sail that had lost its wind. 'I suppose it's possible that Phil has got his wires a bit crossed...'

Then perking up remarkably, Cathy added: 'But I'm sure he'll be delighted to hear that everything is fine. That's all we care about – of course.'

This was my moment to usher Cathy out of the door, or I suspected she'd be hanging around all afternoon. She was already glancing hopefully at her empty glass, which she'd finished almost as soon as I gave it to her. 'Now if you'll excuse me,' I said 'I have things that I really need to get on with.' (That's a useful line I've come across in detective novels. It's what the secretary says when she knows that the detective is trying to get information out of her, and it's more than her job is worth to spill the beans about her boss.)

I was just about to settle down with my book again when the phone rang. And an incredibly nervous sounding young man announced himself as 'Custardjamhollybillybother', or something definitely along those lines.

I had to ask him to repeat this, which he did. Then I had to ask him to repeat it again but this time more slowly. Finally I was able to understand that he was called Constable James. His mission was to find out whether I was Holly. And the reason for his call was something about my brother. When he first mentioned Ryan's name my pulse shot up, in a moment of blind panic. But then I realised that even the most inefficient police force in the world wouldn't ask Constable James to break bad news to someone.

Instead it seemed that the anxious young policeman was trying to find out more about the "phone call" I'd received. What had Ryan said? Were there any clues as to where he was hiding? Had he told me anything of his plans?

So I had to explain to Sherlock Holmes that there had been no phone call as such, just a missed call showing his number. So the Great Detective then wanted to know what evidence I had to show that it was definitely my brother making the call and I told him that

I had no evidence whatsoever.

'I believe what you're saying is that *anybody* could have made this call?' A note of bitter disappointment was slowing Constable James's voice down enough for me to understand what he was saying.

I supposed he was right. Although I don't think it could have been just *anybody*. (It's hard to imagine 82-year-old Mrs Stoker who lives next door to Jane and Martin stealing a mobile from a 14-year-old boy and calling random numbers.)

Constable James didn't seem to have much of a sense of humour. He started trying to explain to me that he was thinking more of a petty criminal of some kind that Ryan might have encountered in the street or on public transport but then stopped abruptly, and laughed with that fake chortling sound people use when they've been very slow in getting a joke that wasn't that funny in the first place.

At that point, there wasn't really much more to be said. Constable James gave me his number and made me promise that I'd call him if Ryan attempted to contact me again. I asked him if there was any way he could trace the call and he said they only do that kind of thing on TV or if it's some really important crime. 'Nice to know that my brother's disappearance doesn't rate as important, I replied, and Constable James nearly choked with embarrassment, explaining over and over again that important meant a situation of national security – a bomb threat or something along those lines. I didn't say anything, it was quite satisfying to hear him squirm.

Finally, Constable James said goodbye but not until he'd reassured me that my brother would probably be 'home very soon' with me and my 'parents'. Which made me worry even more about whether Constable James is capable of reading files.

I took a walk down to the shops and bought a cheap fan in the supermarket. And some extra stuff for supper, so Nathan couldn't complain he was paying to feed my boyf.

By the time Tol turned up I was in a pretty strange mood. I'd had a perfectly good day ruined by idiots, and I was still raging inside that the police seemed to be taking Ryan's disappearance so casually. I'd been taking my mind off all the hassles by planning the lovely romantic evening that Tol and I would spend together. I'd prepared a special recipe I'd seen on one of those programmes where people cook a dinner party for strangers. Where everyone slags off everyone else's cookery skills, bitches about their clothes and pulls nasty faces at the house and all the furniture. But this dish was so delicious that everyone was speechless with admiration.

I'd been saving a stash of chocolate bars that Lucy had given me (must remember to talk to Jane on Sunday) and with the fresh cream I'd just bought (reduced to almost nothing for a quick sale) I could make a special treat for everyone. I could offer Nathan a bowl of this divine iced chocolate soup and then tell him the good news that Lucy was once again free and single. That should make him like me again.

But Nathan said he was in too much of a hurry to eat. He rushed in and out of the flat, grabbed his sports kit and went. 'I'll have some later,' was all he said when I told him about the choccy soup. And just as he was slamming the front door I'm sure I heard him mutter, 'if that Tolobee doesn't eat it all first.'

So I was really pretty stressed out when Tol finally appeared, somewhere around nine o'clock. But I decided to act cool. I didn't want to be one of those girlfriends who whinges all the time and offloads her problems onto her man. He gave me a quick peck on the lips when he arrived and then flopped down onto the sofa. And lit a cigarette. I started to say something but he gave this great big melodramatic sigh. 'Give us a break Hol,' was all he said. So I let him light up – then and there, in the middle of our living room. Where smoking is definitely not allowed. I really will have to talk to him about this tomorrow, but I got the feeling that we'd have a big row if I made an issue of it tonight

I watched him smoke for a minute or two in silence. Just the sight of Tol is enough to make me feel better – even if I'm pretty annoyed with him. Then I told him the plans for the evening. I'd packed us a picnic with veggie flan and my special potato salad. And we had that fab soup I'd spent so long preparing – and storing in a special Tupperware box. But Tol shook his head, 'Sorry babe, I'm just not very hungry. And I'm much too knackered to go anywhere now. Can't we eat it here?'

So we had our "picnic" on the living room floor, kept cool by my new fan. I did most of the eating, although Tol managed a mouthful or two of sweet soup and said it was 'most definitely OK'. I tried to ask him about his day at work, as he'd clearly had a bad time but he didn't want to talk about it. Instead we watched a film on telly and as soon as it finished he fell into bed. I lay for ages beside him but couldn't sleep. So that's why I'm up now and writing this diary.

SATURDAY 15 AUGUST
Day 11 GIA

The last time I wrote this diary, it was the middle of the night and I was watching Tol sleep. Funny really coz that's exactly what I'm doing now – watching someone sleep, except this time it isn't my boyfriend.

It's been such a weird day. Tol woke me up at dawn and insisted it was the perfect time to go for a walk. I'm not that much of an early riser but it did seem like a good plan. We walked by the river for ages, holding hands and making stupid jokes about what names we thought the ducks might call themselves. I even found myself wondering if Tol and I would still be doing this when we're old and retired. It was a weird thought but sort of comforting. I couldn't imagine wanting to do that with anyone else but him.

We had breakfast in a café. I chomped my way through a great big plate of greasy bacon, sausages, eggs and fried potatoes and beans. Tol still wasn't especially hungry (he says he's never hungry when the weather's very hot) so I ate half his scrambled egg as well. I've always had a good appetite, especially after exercise. I'm just lucky that I always seem to burn it off somehow and never put on any weight. Tol was desperate for a cigarette but I said he'd have to go outside and smoke while I finished my food. I wasn't rushing my meal just so he could give himself lung cancer.

After the café Tol wanted to go to the museum. He told me he was in love with a painting there which he knew I would "just adore". I have to admit it wasn't really my kind of painting. Very elaborate and with lots of bright colours and people in floaty clothes staring wistfully into the distance. I think they were meant to be Roman or Greek, but it was hard to tell. They seemed to be waiting for a boat, which was appearing at the side of the picture. I felt sorry for the small black boy with the enormous ostrich feather, whose job it seemed to be to fan everyone and keep them cool. I said this to Tol but he laughed and said I was 'far too practical for my own good,' whatever that meant.

Tol had to go to work at midday and I decided to do a bit of shopping. If this hot weather goes on I'll run out of things to wear. I found a cute little dress in the Oxfam shop for just six pounds. Tiny red flowers on a black background, gathered round the hips and with off-the shoulder sleeves. Quite short, to show off my legs which have got a fantastic tan at the moment (carefully nurtured with high factor suntan lotion that Jane always buys for me and Lucy, coz she's says we'll get skin cancer with all our sunbathing, and she's probably right). In Autumn I can wear it over a black polo-neck and jeans or leggings. I'm always practical when I buy clothes. Well, apart from the red boots. Actually the red boots will look fab with this dress. I may wear the dress for supper at Jane and Martin's tomorrow, so they can see how well I look. I know they have been worrying about me a bit. Jane texts about twice a day to see if I'm OK and I keep telling her I am. I don't think she can quite believe I'm coping as well as I am. Silly really, coz she's part of the reason I'm so good at looking after myself.

Then I went to the hairdressers. Lucy used to cut my hair for me coz she's really good at that sort of thing. But now I'm an independent adult, it felt right to have it done professionally. And there was a dead cheap offer for a cut and blow-dry in one of the local hairdressers. I guess nobody is prepared to sit in a salon in this heat and they're short of customers. But I said I wouldn't need the blow dry so they could make it even cheaper and just give me the cut. They didn't like this much but agreed they would do it. And the stylist was nice enough, especially when I told her that her younger sister was in the year below me at school. She asked what I wanted and I said 'something different' and she asked if this meant that she was allowed to chop some of my hair off. And I thought for a moment before I said yes.

I think the result is pretty cool. She's cut me into this sleek bob which rests on my shoulders, with some feathered bits at the front that come to a point under my jaw line. She said it looked great with the colour of my hair, and that lots of her customers pay to have their hair dyed my colour. Of course, I think it makes my nose look far too big and I've always thought my mouth is a bit of a weird shape, but I know all girls think like this. You have to put those negative thoughts away and focus on your positives; otherwise it can get you down.

I then did some practical stuff like buying a local paper. I'd been moved out for over two weeks now and it was always part of the plan that I'd get a summer job once I was settled in my new place. I have to say that with this heat the thought of working in a stuffy restaurant or sitting on a factory production line doesn't thrill me, but I've never been lazy. Anyway I need to keep putting money away. I've spent far too much lately and I have to be more careful.

I was sitting in a park flicking through the papers when my phone rang and Ryan's name appeared. With trembling fingers I pressed the answer key and tried to sound really casual as I said 'Hello'.

There was silence from the other end but I got the sense that someone was there. So after a few seconds I said, 'Is that you Ryan? I really hope it is, I have so much news to tell you. I've moved into my new place and it's really OK. I'm getting a sofa-bed very soon.'

The silence continued but I knew someone was listening.

'And there's plenty of room. If you came to stay we have a comfy sofa you can sleep on – till the sofa-bed arrives. And you'd like my flatmate, Nathan. He's this cool guy who's really into football, but he likes other sports as well. He plays ice hockey sometimes with the local team – I remember you used to love watching ice hockey when you were a kid and I always said I'd get you lessons when you were old enough. Y' know I could probably afford to pay for some lessons now. I've got some money put away and I've just seen this job in the paper for someone who can operate a computer and answer the phone. And do a bit of filing and that...they say that the right attitude is more important than experience, so they're definitely going to love me...'

I swear I could hear breathing and I knew that breathing was Ryan's. When he was little, my brother used to climb into my bed at night – especially when Mum was having one of her bad days. I'd fallen asleep so many times listening to Ryan's breathing that I knew exactly how it sounded.

'You know what? It would be really cool to meet up. I've missed you little brother. Why don't you text me where you are – and I'll come to you. Or you could come to the flat if you wanted – so I'll text you the address for that as well.' I wanted to leave as many options open as possible, so Ryan didn't feel trapped. For all I knew he could be anywhere in the country, but I had this feeling that he was actually somewhere very close.

I sensed the person on the other end disconnect but that was OK. We had a plan and I knew that Ryan was going to follow it. Immediately I started to text the details of the flat and how to get there by bus, but before I'd finished my phone went ping and a text from Ryan appeared. It simply said *hot drnkz macheen* and I knew immediately where he meant. We'd been travelling back and forwards to see each other from Corrington bus station for ages. If one of us was late, we'd wait by the drinks dispensing machine with our foster carers, until the other turned up. There was a little bench there and it was tucked away, out of the draughts that whistled round that crumbly place in winter. As I got older, Jane and Martin used to wait in the car so that I could meet Ryan on my own. It was quite a special place for both of us.

I wanted to get there as quickly as possible, so I hailed a taxi. It was afternoon rush hour and the traffic was moving so slowly, I thought I'd die from frustration. I had this picture in my head of Ryan sitting on that bench, waiting. And then just giving up and walking away, maybe getting on some bus going hundreds of miles away – somewhere I would never find him. I texted Ryan to say, *Hold on bro, Im cmng*. And to my relief he texted back *OK*.

I almost fell out of the taxi and the driver was quite rude. He thought I was drunk or something. So I didn't give him a tip and he muttered under his breath. Silly man. If he'd played his cards right I'd have paid him to wait for me, so he could take me and my brother somewhere to talk.

I tried to walk calmly through the bus station. There seemed to be hundreds of people getting on and off buses, all hot and bothered and fanning themselves with magazines, or flapping their hands in that silly way that doesn't do anything at all. I wondered if Ryan had travelled in by bus earlier today and where he'd got the fare from. I hoped he wasn't still stealing. But I promised myself I wasn't going to start asking him loads of questions, I didn't want to scare him off. I'd just treat him like he was here on a visit for the time being, while I worked out what to do. I certainly wasn't going to start calling that daft Constable James. And I wasn't quite ready to call Donald either, or Kitty and Craig. Probably the best thing was to leave it and talk to Jane when I had a better idea of what was going on in Ryan's head.

The boy leaning against the wall bore only a slight resemblance to my little brother. He looked smaller somehow, and a lot thinner. His hair was messy and his clothes had that crumpled, slept-in look that could almost pass as fashionable – on an urban make-over photo shoot or something. But the most noticeable thing was the pinched look to his face. His skin was very pale and his cheeks looked hollow. His nose (which like mine has a tendency to be a bit on the big side) looked kind of hawk-like. And he was smoking a cigarette, despite the number of signs warning that this was strictly illegal.

Ryan looked up as I approached. He managed a half-smile and I had to resist the urge to rush up and hug him. I didn't think he'd like that. Instead I walked slowly and made sure that my own smile was welcoming but not too over-the-top. 'Hello little bro,' I said, as casually as if I was just meeting him for a normal contact visit.

'Hey sis,' he replied, dropping the ciggy and giving me a quick hug. But his voice was so quiet I could barely hear him. Then I realised he was trying very hard not to cry. I thought it might be better if I pretended I hadn't noticed.

'Shall we get something to eat?' I said. 'I missed lunch and I'm starving.'

At the mention of food, Ryan's eyes glinted like a wild animal's. I wondered when he'd last had a proper meal.

I watched my kid brother eat a giant burger and two helpings of chips, while I toyed with a bit of salad. I kept talking about this and that while he ate. I told him about Tol but without saying too much – I don't think 14-year-old boys are that much into love and romance. I tried to make a bit of a joke of it. 'I bet you didn't think your sister would ever be that daft,' I said. 'Falling in love with some guy just coz he has the most amazing green eyes. Specially one from a posh background with a really stupid name.'

I expected my brother to react in some way, scoff at me, or something. But he didn't. He just looked at me very, very sadly, like the weight of the whole world was on his shoulders. 'You're lucky, sis,' he said after a while. And added with only the merest hint of a smile, 'I hope he treats you good, though. I'm not in the best shape to sort someone out at the moment.'

This was more like the Ryan I used to know. My sensitive, thoughtful little brother, with that wacky sense of humour I hadn't experienced for a while. And to my horror I burst into tears, right there at the table.

Ryan stopped munching chips for a moment and reached over to pat my hand. 'Oh dear,' he said. 'Being in love has made you a bit soppy, sis.'

I pulled my hand free so I could find a tissue in my handbag. 'Just mega hayfever,' I said. 'The worst I've ever had.'

'You've never had hayfever before, sis.'

'So? That's why this year has been the worst.'

After Ryan had eaten a huge hot fudge sundae and I'd drunk a glass of free tap water (I was trying not to think what all of this food was costing), I started to make some plans. 'Come back with me,' I said. 'Come and stay at the flat – for now. We don't have to tell anyone you're here. Not till you're ready for me to tell them.'

I thought he might resist but Ryan just shrugged and said, 'Sure. Whatever you say, sis.' I realised then that my brother was absolutely exhausted and more than ready to let me look after him. I used more money on a taxi to get us back to St Mark's Crescent, but it was money well spent.

The house was quiet when we arrived. I guess everyone was out enjoying the sunshine, except perhaps Stefan who'd be shut away in his attic room, probably sleeping through the day. I led

Ryan up the stairs and he almost sleep-walked through the front door to my bedroom. I guess not eating for ages and then having a blow-out had made him really sleepy. I didn't mind at all when he fell onto my bed, smelling of sweat and street dust. He let me pull his trainers off for him and the smell of rotten cheddar nearly knocked me sideways. I decided to let him sleep while I went out to buy him some new clothes. I left a note by the bedside saying I'd be back soon, and not to go anywhere. *I luv you little bruv* I wrote at the bottom.

There's a couple of market stalls down the hill and I knew they sold jeans, t-shirts, socks and underwear dead cheaply. Maybe I could also get him some trackies or some pyjamas. The quality wasn't too bad either and my brother's never been into designer labels or anything. All the way there I wanted to call Tol and tell him my wonderful news, but somehow I didn't think this was a good idea. Call me paranoid but I had this feeling that the police might be listening to my calls. Silly really when they couldn't even manage to read my brother's files properly.

Returning with a carrier bag of clothes, I met Nathan on the doorstep. I could see he was really uncomfortable and trying to avoid me, so I decided I had to say something. 'I have some fantastic news,' I told him. 'My brother Ryan just turned up. I hope you don't mind, he's in the flat at the moment. He won't be here for long, just till I can sort him out...'

But Nathan cut me off, by giving me a bear hug that almost lifted me off my feet. 'Man, that is immense!' he said.

It felt like a good time to say something about the last couple of days. 'Look, I'm sorry about Tol,' I said. 'I know I've been a bit thoughtless and all that. Now my brother is here Tol won't be around so much.'

Nathan brushed my comments away with his hand. 'Doesn't matter,' he said. 'What matter is that your bruvver is here. Hey man, we must tell Keesh the good news. You don't mind do you? She won't tell no one – well no one like a social worker or nothing.'

Of course I didn't mind if Keesh and Mel knew that Ryan was here. They'd understand that it was important not to panic my brother by getting the authorities involved. At least until I'd had a chance to discuss it all with Jane.

As soon as Ryan woke up, I insisted he gave me all his clothes and I hustled him into the shower with a stack of fluffy towels. I wanted my new friends to see my little brother looking his best. I stuck all the clothes into a hot wash, together with the sheets my brother had just slept in. Then I started sorting out the sleeping arrangements. I reckoned that Ryan really needed to catch up on sleep, so he'd better have my bed for the moment. And I would sleep on the couch in the living room. I could go and stay with Tol in the top flat, but I felt uneasy about the thought of leaving my little brother alone. I didn't want him waking up and suddenly deciding to vanish again.

I realised then that I hadn't texted Tol all afternoon, so I sent him a quick message: *Some v g news. Can't w8 2 tel u.* And almost immediately another text came back: *Hey babes, not round 2nite. Catch u 2moro Luv u T xxxx*

My first reaction was deep disappointment, then I realised I was also quite angry. He hadn't mentioned anything about working late. But then we had spent the morning together so maybe I was just being a bit greedy. Anyway, I had more important things to think about. So I just texted back saying *Don't wrk 2 hard. And dnt 4gt we gng 2 supper with J and M 2moro. Lucy ded xctd bout meetin u. Luv u 2 H xxxxxx*

I'd been texting Lucy regularly since our visit to the pool, and wondered now if I should tell her about Ryan. But it wasn't fair to expect her to keep it a secret from her mum and dad. I'd tell her tomorrow when I told Jane.

Almost immediately a reply came back – *Sorry babes hd 4gt.*
Nt sure can mk it.

Without thinking, I texted back: *U betr!!!! U promzd me. Im ded*
angry wiv u. He should know how much this meant to me. How
would it look if I turned up at Jane and Martin's saying, 'Hey, you
know this amazing guy I told you about, who you cooked that
special supper for because he doesn't eat meat? Well, he isn't
coming. Why? Oh I don't know. Just couldn't be bothered I expect.'
That probably wasn't fair and it was probably because Tol's boss
wanted him to take photos of drug smugglers or gun dealers
unloading boxes in the docks. (I still really don't know what Tol's
work is about but it sounds quite dangerous stuff.) And I knew he
needed the money coz this morning he said he was a bit short and
asked if I was OK for me to pay for breakfast, but the visit to Jane
and Martin's was special.

Fortunately a text came back saying, *Hey babes, sozzee...dint*
mean 2 make u mad. Will come wiv u.What should I wer? T xxx

So at least that was one problem sorted. I wasn't going to have
to dump my gorgeous boyfriend and spend the next few days
trying not to cry in front of my brother. Tol wasn't perfect and he
could be a bit irritating sometimes, but I knew that I really did love
him and splitting up was an incredibly painful thought.

Ryan and I had supper in my room. I made us enormous baked
potatoes with grated cheese and lots of healthy salad. Ryan turned
up his nose at the salad but I told him he wasn't getting any of my
delicious pudding unless he got some vitamin C into him. He said I
sounded 'just like Mum'.

Then he asked me, 'D'you ever think about Mum, Hols?'

I was about to say yes, all the time, but then I stopped to think
about it. How many times have I mentioned her in this diary?

'Not that much really – if I'm honest,' I told Ryan. 'I think it's
because it upsets me to think about her. So I try not to.'

Ryan looked a bit surprised by my answer. After a while he said, 'I think about her all the time. Like four or fives times a day or something. And I think about Dad – your dad, not my dad...an' what he's doin' in America.'

I told him then about my dreams. Especially about the one where he was trying to get to America in the frozen meat van.

'I'm sorry, sis,' he said, when I'd finished describing it. 'I didn't mean to upset you.'

'Yeah, well you're my brother and however much grief you give me I still love you – even when I also want to wring your scrawny little neck,' I said, trying to keep it light. But I put out my hand and he held onto it, really tightly, which reminded me suddenly of Simon at Jane and Martin's.

'Anyway,' I continued. 'You're back with me now and I'm going to keep you safe.'

'Thanks sis,' he said, and then after a moment very quietly: 'I never stole nothin' again sis. You mustn't worry I'm like a criminal or anything.'

It was a relief to hear this. I read in one of Jane's books that nearly ten per cent of kids in care have a conviction or have been in serious trouble with the police. My brother and I are never going to be part of any statistics – if I can help it. (Well, maybe the ones that say there's a rise in the number of care leavers going on to FE.)

There were a million other things I wanted to know but I thought I'd better not push it. So I just said, 'Glad to hear it,' and changed the subject to what we should watch on TV.

During the evening there was a gentle knock on the bedroom door and when I went to answer it, Nathan was standing there looking awkward. 'Wondered if your bruvver needed clothes or anything?' he asked timidly. I beckoned him into the room and made introductions. Ryan looked a bit wary at first but Nathan was even more nervous, twisting his fingers together and shuffling his feet. And some of the old Ryan started to appear, as grimacing, he showed Nathan the pyjamas I'd bought for him.

'Man, those are evil!' Nathan shook his head at the very practical looking pair of pyjamas I'd bought for £3 from the market stall. It was only listening to Ryan and Nathan complaining about women having 'no sense nor nothing' that I realised why the items had been so cheap. They bore the logo of a football team that apparently nobody in their right mind would want to be associated with.

Then somehow Nathan was sitting down to watch TV with us. I was soon the subject of an ongoing joke – with Nathan shaking his head every now and then and chuckling about the offending pyjamas, and Ryan gradually relaxing enough to tell Nathan about some of the clothes I'd bought him when he was a kid. (In my defence, I was only nine at the time and I didn't know that boys and girls wore different jeans.) This was definitely the old Ryan – who could keep people entertained for ages with his comedy routines.

At around 10pm Ryan showed signs of starting to flake. Nathan said goodnight – but reappeared a minute later with a large red t-shirt. 'You sleep better in dis,' he said, thrusting it into Ryan's hand and beating a quick retreat. After he'd gone, Ryan showed it to me. It bore the emblem of Nathan's ice-hockey team.

I explained to Ryan that he would be sleeping in my room and I'd be camping down in the living room. To my amazement he asked, 'Can't we both sleep in here, sis – I'd be OK on the floor?'

I was about to say that it would be far too hot and we'd probably need the fan on all night, but I noticed the pleading look in his eyes. I got the impression my little brother had seen some pretty scary things recently, and he wasn't too keen on being by himself. But I made him take the bed, and I borrowed some cushions from the living room sofa to make myself a mattress.

I knocked on Nathan's door first, just to check he didn't mind. 'No prob,' he replied. 'Your kid brother is cool, man,' and then after a moment's slight embarrassment he added, 'And your hair is cool too.'

So I'm here now, sitting at my desk by the window, writing this diary with the light of the streetlights from over the road. Ryan slept like a baby for a while, but now he's tossing and turning in his sleep. He's making little whimpering animal noises and I'm wondering whether to wake him up and see if he's OK.

5am

I can't sleep now for thinking about all the things Ryan told me. I wish I could find the people who do such things to kids and torture them to death – very, very slowly. I've never felt so angry and so protective in my life. I understand now why people murder someone who's killed or harmed someone that matters to them. I've told Ryan that he must tell the police about these people but he's not really sure where they are. He'd met one of them outside a church and the guy had offered him some food, and he accepted it because he thought the man was something to do with the church. And he doesn't remember much about what happened after that. He thinks they doped him, and he only half remembers someone shoving him into a van. When he came round all these men were there and doing horrible things to him – things he can't bear to tell me about – till someone forced him to drink something again, and it seemed like days had passed before he became conscious again. He remembers something about being driven somewhere in the van and a house with lots of stairs, and being kept locked in a room at the top. And lots of different men coming and going – and someone taking photos.

And he vaguely remembers the night he couldn't bear it any more and kicked some guy hard in the nuts and ran out of the room, and down the stairs. And fortunately there was no one around and his coat was hanging up near the front door – with his mobile still in his "secret inside pocket" (after he got mugged last time he'd made sure that his phone was somewhere no one would find it) and he managed to unlock the front door and run out into the street. And to keep on running and running and running, until finally he came to a little wood, where it was so dark he thought that nobody could find him. And he hid in a ditch under some bramble bushes all night, too scared to sleep.

At dawn he said that the wood was a bit friendlier and he spotted some berries he thought were safe to eat, and he sucked moisture from the dew on the grass. But he was too frightened to move from the wood all day in case the men were out looking for him in their van. So he stayed another night in the wood, but by the second day he was so hungry and thirsty he couldn't stay there any more. He decided to go somewhere where there would be lots of people – so if the men came again, he could call for help. I asked him why he didn't phone someone but he said he tried to call me, but I didn't answer. And he was afraid the phone might run out so he'd saved it as long as he could. And when I asked why he didn't knock on the first door he came to and tell someone to call the police, he just shook his head. 'They wouldn't of believed me,' was what he said.

He asked an old man which was the best way to the shops and the man said there was a town about five miles away and he'd best get a bus, but he said he had no money and he was used to walking. So someone else told him some directions and he spent the day walking to the town. There were lots of people out having picnics, so he hung around a bit and when some families dumped their rubbish, he went through the bins and found some bits of food he could eat. He also found a half-empty bottle of fizzy water under a park bench – which he tested first to make sure it was really water and not something dangerous or disgusting.

In the town there was a train station and Ryan knew that he had to get a train to somewhere like a big city where there were connections to other cities. He managed to follow these two rather drunk women with buggies onto the platform by looking like he was just one more of their scruffy, grumpy kids. When the guard came round for the tickets he went to the toilets and made throwing up noises, really loudly, so the guard didn't bother to hang around.

At Manchester he had changed trains, using a similar trick. This time by hanging around the edge of a big party of overseas students and crawling under the legs of some of the girls when the ticket inspector came. The students seemed to think it was funny and they hadn't reported him to the inspector. They probably couldn't say "strange, smelly boy" in English, so that was also maybe why he got away with it.

He said he'd arrived at the train station the night before last. He'd walked around for a bit then gone down to the bus station. There was always someone sitting or sleeping in the waiting room there, so he knew he probably wouldn't get chucked out. A tramp offered him some of her whisky and a street beggar bought him a mug of tea at the all-night café. (He'd watched very carefully as the guy bought the tea. He was wary now of anyone putting anything into his drinks, but he was too tired and thirsty to say no to the tea or the whisky.) And he'd stayed at the bus station all morning, trying to get up enough courage to call me, coz he thought I'd be 'really mad' with him, and coz he felt so ashamed and dirty because of the things the men had done to him.

At that point, I wrapped my arms around my little brother. 'You've nothing to be ashamed of,' I said, squeezing him so tightly he had to tell me that he couldn't really breathe. 'Those men – they are the ones who should be ashamed. They are animals! No, worse than animals. They are scum-of-the-earth monsters who should be ashamed to live.'

But Ryan looked at me with tears in his eyes. 'Maybe it's a punishment,' he said, after a while, ' coz of what I am.'

I started to say that stealing a purse didn't make him a monster but I realised this wasn't what he was talking about. 'Because I'm a gay – a queer, a poof,' he said, very quietly, and started to cry.

Jane has listened to children telling her all sorts of terrible and secret things and she says that it's important to do a lot of listening, and to ask very gentle questions that won't make the child think you're judging them. I tried to imagine I was Jane as I said, very calmly: 'Why do you say that, Ryan?'

'Because it's true – or maybe it's true. It's what the kids at school say I am,' Ryan looked at me, his tear-filled eyes so full of pain that it broke my heart to see him suffering like this.

Some of the kids at my school used to call any boy who was into art or drama or stuff like poetry "gay". It didn't mean they necessarily thought they liked other boys, just that they were "soft" or not macho enough. I don't really like that they use that word to mean something bad. When you've lived with as much prejudice as me and Ryan have lived with, about our mum being "a looney" and about us being "kids that nobody wanted", you get kinda sensitive about other people's feelings. There was even some talk about it on the news, about some radio broadcaster using that word and nobody seemed to think it was that bad. Even some of the gay people thought it was OK to use it. But Ryan wasn't into art or drama or poetry, he was into football and video games and all the stuff many teenage boys are into.

'I don't care what you are – whether you are gay or not,' I said holding my brother by the shoulders and looking deep into his eyes. 'People are who they are and that's all that matters. And you're my brother and I love you more than anyone else in the world.'

Ryan looked at me warily. 'But what if I grow up to be like those men? What if they picked on me because they guessed I was like them?'

'Why would you? Being gay – or thinking you might be gay, doesn't mean you'll grow up to be a paedophile. Those men were paedophiles coz they are adults who want to have sex with children. Being gay doesn't mean you want to have sex with children. No way!'

'But what if I fancy a boy – or boys of my own age? Which I'm not saying that I do...'

'It's OK. Fancying someone of your own age is fine,' I said. 'What absolutely isn't OK is fancying kids when you're adult – and doing stuff to them.'

Jane had told me and Lucy about this adult/kid stuff when we'd had an eleven-year-old girl living in our house who kept flirting in this really disgusting way with Martin, and any man who came to the house. Lucy and I asked Jane what we should do to stop her behaving like that. Jane said that this girl had probably had lots of inappropriate stuff done to her by adult men, since she was very young. So she didn't know how to form healthy relationships with other people. Jane said the best thing we could do was help the girl to value herself and to value her body. So me and Lucy were very prim and proper for a while, not wearing short skirts and not flirting with any boys at all, when the girl was around. I don't know if it helped, but we wanted to show the girl that we valued ourselves and didn't see ourselves as "sex objects".

'Craig hates poofs. He says that the army makes you tough,' Ryan blurted out suddenly. And the pieces of the jigsaw started to come together – why my brother had been running away from his foster carers.

'Are you sure about that?' I asked, carefully, once again trying to pretend I was Jane. I could imagine Craig being a bit old-style in his thinking. But I couldn't imagine that anyone who was as gentle with Lewis as Craig was could be a total meat-head.

Ryan nodded. 'Yeah, he said he can't stand campness – he doesn't like watching men dressing up in women's clothes and all that stuff. So I know he'd hate me if he knew I was...not that I definitely am or anything...'

'I don't think "camp" is the same thing as "gay",' I said, a bit unsure now of what I was talking about. 'I think camp means sort of flouncy – a bit girly in some way.'

Ryan looked uncertain. 'So Craig would only hate me if I was a camp – sort of girly and giggly like?'

'I don't think Craig would hate you whatever you were. He's been worried sick about you going missing. But maybe he needs to be more careful about what he says. We need to talk to Donald about all of this,' I said.

Ryan tensed like a rabbit in the headlights. 'No!'

'OK,' I said, smoothing the hair on my brother's forehead, like I used to when he was a baby and couldn't sleep. 'But what if I talk to Jane tomorrow?'

Again Ryan tensed. 'Not yet,' he said. 'I don't want no one to know. Nothing at all about none of it. Can't we keep it secret, sis – just between us? Then I can just go back to Kitty and Craig when I feel a bit better, and no one has to know a thing. Promise me sis, you won't tell no one what I told you?'

I promised, but I knew it was a promise I couldn't keep for very long. I knew that Ryan was going to need help to get over his terrible experiences at the hands of those men. But at that moment I was far too scared I'd lose him. If he thought for a minute that I was going to involve anyone else, then I was sure he'd run away again.

So I'm just going to have to play it very carefully, looking after him until he's ready. It's a good job that I have a lot of experience of taking care of myself and that I'm so capable. Someone else in my situation would be absolutely terrified and just panic and mess it all up.

MONDAY 17 AUGUST (6am)
—Don't know what day this is but think it's Day 13 of my G/A phase

I can't sleep again. I thought things couldn't get much worse but yesterday they just did. I've had this mega bust-up with Jane and Lucy and I don't think I'll ever forgive either of them. As if I didn't already have enough to worry about, now I can't even talk to my best friend or the woman I used to think of as my second mum. And even my boyfriend's being a bit snippy with me. It just shows there's no one in the world you can really trust, unless they're your own flesh and blood. And I'm not even sure if I can trust Ryan at the moment. Well at least not to run away, or something. He's been so down and moody, like he regrets what he told me the other night and doesn't trust me not to tell someone. I've tried to be very patient and reassure him that I won't do anything without his permission but he looks at me so distrustfully. Foster kids get told a lot of promises through their lives, but so often people let them down. Our mum swore she'd never let us be taken into care, but it still happened.

I stayed at home with Ryan all morning but he didn't seem to want me around. I also had to wake Nathan up and explain that if he hadn't already told Keesh and Mel, then maybe it was best not to. I told a very bleary-eyed Nathan that things were 'a bit complicated' and my brother needed some time before he was ready for anyone to know he was here. Nathan said he hadn't told anyone else yet, but he suggested that maybe I should talk to Phil or Cathy. 'They good people, they'd understand,' he reassured me. He also suggested that sooner or later they'd probably find out. Which is why I dropped a note into Phil and Cathy's office which read: *Hope it's OK, one of my brothers is staying with me for a few days. His foster mum got taken into hospital very suddenly and his social worker asked if it was OK if he could come to me.*

That, I thought, should confuse them. I bet they don't know how many brothers I have and they probably haven't even been told that my younger brother has gone missing. But just in case, I knew I needed a cunning plan to keep them off the scent. Not that I could imagine Phil or Cathy ever making decent bloodhounds – they'd be fooled by the first toy rabbit someone waved at them from behind a hedge.

Nathan lent Ryan some books and DVDs about football and ice-hockey and there was some stuff on my iPod that my brother seemed to like, so at least he kept himself occupied. It gave me some time to do some housework and a bit of reading.

I explained to Ryan that I had to go over to Jane and Martin's for supper. I'd also arranged to meet Tol at the bus stop, round the corner from their house. I would introduce Ryan and Tol soon, but I wasn't sure that Ryan was quite ready to meet anyone new. Nathan was quiet and easy to get along with, and Ryan seemed to feel comfortable around him, but Tol could be a bit of an extrovert and that probably wasn't what Ryan needed at the moment.

I got to the bus stop early, as I was excited about seeing Tol. I hadn't seen him for nearly two days and I missed him something rotten. I was wearing the new dress I'd bought in the Oxfam shop – with the red boots. It's a bit shorter than I remembered but it does

show off my suntanned legs to their best advantage. I used to be
self-conscious about boys looking at my legs but I love it when Tol
pays me compliments, and I was feeling pretty good about myself.

Of course, Tol was late. Well very late, actually. We were due at
Martin and Jane's no later than 6pm coz the young kids get hungry.
So I'd said to Tol that he must meet me by 5.45 at the very latest.
Instead he turns up at 6.20, running and all hot and flustered. But
it's hard to stay cross with someone who turns up with a white
silk shirt stuck to their awesomely muscled stomach. So instead I
kissed him and that made us even later.

Jane tried not to look cross when we arrived after 6.40. She
said she hoped we didn't mind but she'd let the younger children
eat, and me and Martin and Lucy and Tol would have our meal
separately. She took us out to the garden where Lucy was playing
with a toddler in the paddling pool. Lucy passed the child over to
Jane and gave me a big hug. Before checking out Tol from head to
toe, and finally saying with a big smile on her face, 'You must be
Tol. Hol has told me all about you.'

Tol did that stupid thing he does with kissing girl's hands and
Lucy absolutely loved it. She giggled like a three-year-old.

Jane had to go in to put the toddler to bed and to get the older
kids into their pyjamas so they could stay up and watch a DVD
while we ate. Lucy and I sat down on the chairs but Tol started
to wander around the garden, as though he was restless. Martin
appeared and gave me a big hug and shook hands with Tol, and
then appeared with big tumblers of his homemade lemonade,
which is sour and a bit sugary all at the same time, and perfect on
a hot day.

Martin asked me lots of questions about the new place and
Lucy asked when she was coming over to stay, and I said, 'Soon
as I get everything settled and buy that sofa-bed,' which is what
I've been telling her since I moved. At first I didn't really want Lucy

staying at my new place – not until I felt everything was exactly how I wanted it. But now I can't have her over – not with Ryan there. Lucy looked a bit hurt but I will explain to her sometime, when everything with Ryan is sorted out.

I changed the subject and asked how everything was going with them. Martin sighed and rolled his eyes. 'Kids everywhere Holly, even in cupboards and under the bed.'

It turned out that as well as Simon and the toddler I'd just seen, there were also twin girls staying for a couple of nights. 'We got asked to take an emergency placement – only for three nights and Mum just couldn't say no, although there weren't really enough bedrooms to go round. I'm on a put-up bed in the study so the twins can have my room. They've already been here two days longer than they were meant to stay. So you really need to have me over soon, Hol!'

Poor Lucy, I'd already forgotten how bad it could get. There are limits on how many children foster carers are allowed to take, but when an emergency situation occurs the social workers seem to forget about this. Summer holidays are usually a bad time. Foster carers go off on their own holidays and they can't always take their foster kids with them, coz you're not allowed to take someone else's child out of the country without filling in millions of forms and getting the permission of a court, or something like that. And then there are kids whose parents can't really cope at the best of times, who just completely lose it when the kids are home from school all day long. So those kids all need someone to look after them while plans get made for their future. Which is why there's always a house full of kids at Jane and Martin's during the summer holiday.

While we were talking, Tol had wandered down to the bottom of the garden. I thought at first he'd gone to look at the rabbits or that Boots the cat was there, but I soon realised he was checking his mobile – and making some calls. I hoped Martin hadn't noticed coz it looked pretty rude, even if it was urgent work stuff.

Eventually Jane called to say that food was served. Tol was still on the phone so I went down to tell him to hurry up. 'Give me a mo!' he almost snapped at me, turning his back so I couldn't see who he was talking to. Terrific, I thought, one stroppy boyfriend. That's going to go down really well with my foster family.

But by the time we sat down for supper, Tol was his normal chatty self. Almost too chatty if anything. He started asking Jane all these questions about why she fostered and if she didn't get bored of other people's kids. And then he launched into this long story about his own childhood and his relationship with his mother, which was a bit too full-on really – the same stuff he'd told me our first night together. But I think Jane has that effect on people: they trust her and want to tell her things they'd never tell anyone else.

I was trying to watch Lucy to see what she ate, but she seemed totally distracted by Tol. She hadn't taken her eyes off him once since we sat down and it was hard to tell whether she was deliberately not eating or whether she was so mesmerised by my handsome boyf that she'd forgotten about food. Either way, I knew I had to have a quiet word with Jane in the kitchen later, which made me start worrying about Ryan. I'd cooked him a big plate of chips and beans at midday and then left him with a huge pile of cheese and pickle sandwiches and a packet of chocolate biscuits. He was still eating like a starved wolf, which I thought had to be a good sign that he was getting a bit healthier. I so wanted to ask Jane's advice and I was starting to think that maybe it would be OK to tell her.

I knew I'd promised my brother that I wouldn't tell Jane – but that was only because I was terrified he might run off. Some promises just have to be broken and the more I thought about it, the more I realised that this was one promise I couldn't keep.

Then, suddenly, a really horrible thought hit me. And I wondered why it hadn't occurred to me before. What if those men had given Ryan some kind of disease? I felt quite sick at the idea of my little brother being infected by HIV. I needed to get him tested as quickly as possible.

After that I found it hard to eat anything. And I noticed, looking round the table that I wasn't the only one. Lucy was still gaping at Ptolemy while toying with a forkful of mushroom risotto. While Tol seemed to have eaten nothing at all. Poor Jane, I thought, she'd gone to all that effort to make a special meal and now nobody was eating it. Except Martin of course, who can always eat. If Martin was on a sinking ship like the *Titanic*, he'd be in the dining room when all the other passengers were rushing to get into the lifeboats, filling his pockets with all the leftovers. Because he just hates to see wasted food. He'd probably get left behind and be one of those people who was spotted floating on a bit of driftwood when the rescue boats arrived. He'd still be munching on a chicken drumstick when they found him.

I forced a few more mouthfuls down, trying not to think about Ryan. And trying to listen to the conversation Martin was attempting to start with Tol. What exactly was it that Tol did for a job, Martin wanted to know. Did he work for just one private detective or a number of them? Was it just photography he did or did he do a bit of "sleuthing" (which was how Martin put it). Was the work anything like they showed it on TV – where people sat around for hours in cars, pretending to read a newspaper, and then something really exciting happened and the police closed in with sirens and shotguns? I knew that Martin was just being curious (Martin's always interested in other people's lives) but Tol seemed to find it hard to answer any of his questions. His answers got more and more obtuse until he almost snapped that of course it was 'nothing like they showed it on TV – just a boring job, OK?'

There was a moment's silence around the table, with Martin, Lucy and Jane looking a bit shocked. And I couldn't really blame them. Tol was being hyper-sensitive. I know he thinks everybody's family are like his parents, but I'd tried to tell him Jane and Martin aren't like that. They just accept everyone for what they are. And just as he always does, Martin took Tol's comment on the chin (I guess he's used to much ruder stuff from some of the kids we've fostered).

'So what you're saying is this isn't your perfect job, then Ptolemy?' he asked, all laid back and friendly (he even got the pronunciation right with the E sound at the end). 'So tell me, what would your perfect job be?'

Tol regarded him warily for a minute so I jumped in. 'It's OK Tol,' I said quickly, 'Martin is very supportive of people who want to be artists and writers and things like that…they've always encouraged me to be anything I want to be. They're not like your parents.'

Something clicked behind Martin's eyes and he chipped in hastily with a comment about how he'd always wanted to be an actor when he was a kid and how he couldn't really understand why he'd ended up in town planning. Then he went on to ask Tol if he'd seen any of my pictures, and didn't Tol think I was rather good?

My boyfriend still looked a bit wary, as though he suspected this was some big test or competition, and any minute now Martin would announce the score. But he did warm up a bit as the conversation turned to a discussion about some art programme on the telly, where members of the public were being asked to vote for their all-time favourite paintings. Martin said he could only think of three paintings – the *Mona Lisa*, the *Sunflowers* and the *Haywagon* – and to be honest he didn't like any of those very much. And Lucy laughed and said that even she could name more famous paintings than that. Then Jane said that she wished she could paint and that she loved those 17th-century Dutch paintings showing the insides of houses, with lots of black-and-white tiles on the floor and people cooking or sewing – but what intrigued her most was that you could often see through a window or a reflection in the mirror, and there was a feeling that a whole world was happening, which you could only catch a glimpse of.

Tol said he had a different favourite almost every month. Sometimes it was something very modern but at the moment he was in love with the Victorian painting in the city gallery – the one he'd shown me earlier in the week. It did sound a bit pretentious when he said that but Lucy was gazing at him again, as though he'd said the most profound thing ever. I felt a bit irritated with her then. This was my boyf she was ogling like a lovesick cow.

I helped Martin clear away the plates while Lucy went to help Jane in the kitchen. Lucy appeared a few minutes later carrying an enormous chocolate gateau. 'T'dah!' she announced, placing it on the table. 'This is one I made earlier.'

Jane who was standing behind her cleared her throat.

'OK, Mums – so you made the cake but I did all the bits with cream and cherries,' Lucy said, popping a finger in her mouth to suck off some of the goo which had fallen onto her hands as she carried it. I watched carefully. But there was no look of sudden horror, no shock reaction as she realised what she'd done. Nothing at all that made me think that Lucy was a girl with a serious eating disorder. But as she dished out large helpings to everyone, I wondered if this meant that she was planning to pig out then make herself sick afterwards. (Sometimes I wish I didn't notice things. Then I wouldn't have to walk around with my head stuffed full of other people's problems.)

To my relief, Tol ate a bit of the gateau. Well, only a very little bit, but at least he told Lucy that it tasted delicious and he wished that he didn't lose his appetite so badly in hot weather. So Lucy

was happy enough with that. And bored Tol with a whole range
of stories about how she'd been hopeless at cooking at school
and how her parents had been so nice about eating all sorts of
disgusting things she'd brought home.

'It wasn't that bad, as far as I remember,' Jane said.

But Martin grimaced. 'That's because you always made me eat
most of it. Don't you remember those buns she made that were like
rocks?'

'I do. But weren't they rock cakes?'

'My point exactly!' Martin spluttered through a mouthful of
cream. 'They were meant to be fairy cakes or little sponges –
something light and fluffy. You put one in my lunchbox every day
for a week, and I don't think you tasted a single one.'

Jane smiled. 'And wasn't it soon after that you started to make
all the packed lunches?'

'You see! I knew my cooking had a purpose!' Lucy was waving
a fork about in glee. Her cheeks were flushed and her eyes were
shining. She looked the picture of blooming health. As I watched,
I saw Jane catch her daughter's eye for just one second, and some
secret signal passed between them before Jane moved hurriedly
towards the door.

'And now – if you'll excuse me, I have to go and make sure the
children aren't tearing up the living room. It's been a bit too quiet
in there for my liking...and probably way past the twins' bedtime.
I'll be back in ten mins for coffee. Lucy will you sort out drinks and
find out what the little 'uns want?'

'I'll help you,' I said and went into the kitchen, to switch on
the kettle. I could hear Martin and Tol having a civilised sounding
conversation in the front room, so Tol was obviously starting to
unwind.

'Two teas, two coffees, a glass of water for your *divine*
boyfriend and a cup of milk for Kylie – or was it Katie? Anyway, the

other one wants orange juice and Simon says you'll know what he wants? D'you Hols? I never thought you had much time for him.'

Sometimes you want to say something so badly that you get it all wrong. I didn't mean to sound angry with Lucy but my words got jumbled up. 'Why did you lie to me Lucy?' I heard myself snapping at her.

'I didn't exactly lie,' Lucy looked shocked by my reaction. I wasn't ready to tell anyone Hol...I really wasn't...I only told Mum the other day – after you told me how worried she was.'

'So you let me think you had bulimia or something? You knew about that girl who died in my children's home. She got anorexia and she never recovered. You know how much I worry about that happening to someone I love...'

Lucy shook her head. 'It wasn't like that Hol – you have to believe me. I wasn't putting it on. I felt so sick all the time and every time I ate I knew I'd probably spew up. But I'd made up my mind that I was going to get rid of the baby, so I didn't want to tell anyone about it. And you seemed so busy Hol, with all your own stuff going on. I just didn't want anyone to know.'

'So why didn't you tell me? After you told your mum? I'm supposed to be your best friend after all!'

'Mum said I shouldn't tell you over the phone – that it was better to tell you face to face. Mum's been really brilliant, you know. She says I should wait a little while and think it all through – she's made me an appointment with this pregnancy advisor so I can get some "independent" advice, coz honestly I really don't know what I want Hols. I mean I love the idea of having a baby and all that, and I know I'd be a great mum, but with all the kids we've had here... I mean I know it's tough being a single mum. And I don't want to be a burden to Mum and Dad. They have enough with the foster kids.'

Typical Lucy, putting everyone's needs before her own. I didn't know whether to shake her or hug her. But I was still pretty angry that she had lied to me at the swimming pool. 'You could have trusted me Luce – you know you could! I'm really mad that you didn't tell me the truth!'

The colour in Lucy's cheeks suddenly got a whole lot redder. 'And you know what, Hols? I'm pretty mad with you too! I've really needed you these last few weeks but you've not been there for me. I've been texting and calling you every day, asking about your brother and asking if there's anything you need. But you hardly ever bother to pick up or return my messages. And Mum and Dad have been worrying about you as well. But you move out and it's like you don't want anything more to do with us. You've hardly bothered to get in touch with us at all. You meet this new bloke and it's like we don't matter any more.'

I knew pregnant women have mood swings but that was crazy. But I wasn't going to get carried away. 'Don't talk about things you don't understand,' I told Lucy very firmly. 'You've no idea what it's like having to go and live on your own and look after yourself. You've got your mum and dad behind you all the way – and even when you're stupid enough to get yourself knocked up, despite the advice everyone gave you, they still stand behind you. You don't know how lucky you are!'

Lucy turned to me, hand on hips, and started to wag her finger at me, like I was some naughty child she'd found stealing sweets. 'Get over yourself Holly! Sure my mum and dad are standing behind me and you know what? They'd do just the same thing for you too, if it ever happened to you. Although you're always Miss Bloody Perfect and *of course* you wouldn't ever get caught like I did, coz that's what my mum and dad are like – really caring people.'

Lucy and I hadn't rowed for ages. I'd forgotten how carried away she can get when she thinks she's in the right. And she continued just as ferociously. 'Just think about that poor kid who came here last year, Hols – about the same age as me now. Her mum and dad were something big in TV and she'd been to a really posh school. But when she wouldn't get rid of her baby they told her that she had to move out. They actually got their driver to dump her at social services! And they did this interview with the papers telling everyone that she'd turned into a wild child and they couldn't cope with her no more...

'So don't you tell me that you've always had it harder than everyone else Holly! Mum told me there are still kids who get pushed out of foster care when they reach 16 or 17 and have to live by themselves, coz their foster families can't afford to keep them. Nobody forced you out Holly. You chose to go and leave us.'

How could Lucy understand what it was like to be in my position? Sure, Jane and Martin had been like parents to me and she'd been like my sister. But the point was that she wasn't really my sister. And I wasn't hers. The only person who had the right to call me "sister" was waiting for me now back at my place – frightened and ashamed. Because the only stability he'd ever had in his life was me, and he'd been failed by foster carers, and social workers and police and all sorts of people who should have been there to protect him had let him down, and he'd ended up on the streets where he'd been the victim of something that would probably scar him for life. So when it came down to it, the only person in the world he could really trust was me.

And I wondered then why I'd ever thought about breaking my promise to Ryan and talking to Jane. Jane was part of the system. She was kind and caring and sensible, but she was also bound by all sorts of policies and procedures and she'd tell me that she had to report Ryan's reappearance – in case she got struck off as a foster carer or something.

I stormed out of the kitchen but almost immediately bumped

into Jane, who was coming down the stairs. She had a really concentrated look on her face but I don't think she'd overheard anything of the row between Lucy and me. But as soon as she saw me, she smiled – and beckoned me into her study, and closed the door behind us.

'It's OK, I worked it out for myself – about Lucy's pregnancy.' I told Jane, not really caring if that sounded a bit brutal. 'Anyway, I know that Lucy's told you – so there's really nothing to talk about.'

But Jane just nodded. She was regarding me with a look that made me really uneasy.

'Holly,' she said putting her hand on my arm. 'This Ptolemy seems a nice enough boy. But how much do you really know about him?'

What was it with everyone recently – trying to tell me how I should live my life? I thought Jane had more faith in me than that. Besides she's not my mother and if she thinks she can start telling me who I should or shouldn't see she was completely wrong. Just coz she liked Sean a lot doesn't mean she has the right to criticise Tol.

'What do you mean?' I asked, bristling with anger which I was no longer trying to hide.

I could see that Jane was weighing up the situation; she's always careful with her words. But I was just getting more and more irate inside. Eventually she said, 'Holly, I hate to say this but I think it's possible this boy may be a bit of a drug addict.'

I couldn't believe what I was hearing. How could Jane be so stupid! Did she think that everyone with floppy hair, who looks a bit like a romantic poet or whatever, has a drug problem?

'He's not!' is all I managed to say.

'I'm really sorry to mention this Holly – but you can be a bit... well, naive about these things...You've always been so focused yourself, so not interested in drugs and drink and all that stuff...'

'Yeah but I've hardly been a saint! Lots of my friends do a bit of blow and drink too much... Sean was always rolling joints when I first met him, if you really want to know.'

Jane looked me straight in the eyes. 'I'm not talking about the occasional bit of dope, Holly. I suspect this boy is using heroin – quite regularly.'

'And how would you know?' I almost spat my reply. 'You're not exactly *down with the kids*, Jane. Whatever you may think!'

'Because Rob – my own son – had a habit for a while, got in with some older lads from school, and after a time you can tell these things. You just know from being around someone.'

That was the first time I'd heard any mention of Rob's problem. I've met Jane and Martin's oldest son lots of times, of course. He came round with his wife and kids and he didn't look like the kind of guy who used to get wasted smoking or injecting smack.

'There are signs like mood swings,' Jane continued, 'and something about the eyes – very intense one moment, sort of not with you the next – and the lack of appetite. Your friend hardly touched his food.

'We got Rob off it in the end. Well, he got himself off with a bit of support from us. It's one of the reasons we decided to foster; we felt we had some experience of dealing with problems. It's why we try to never judge other parents.'

'Yeah, but now you're judging Ptolemy! OK, I think he smokes a bit of weed, but that doesn't mean he's shooting up or anything... you must be mixing up the signs.'

'Holly, I can't believe you're talking like this. You've always said you wouldn't tolerate being around anyone with any kind of drug habit. You used to say that anyone who needed drugs to keep them going was a loser.'

The same words that Mel had used to describe Ptolemy...And yes, I had said that thing about drug users to Jane. But that was when I was less mature about these things. Anyway, that wasn't the point. 'None of this means that he's a smackhead!' I snapped at Jane, more ferociously than I intended.

'Holly, I'm not saying that, I'm just worried...'

But I'd heard enough. I loved Tol and I wasn't going to let Jane screw up my relationship with her silly paranoia. Robert's nearly 30 now, so she probably doesn't remember that much about the signs. We did drugs ed at school and we had to do research about it for this debate we had with the grammar school. I'm not sure some of the stuff Jane was saying was right. Thinking back, she was a bit weird about Sean when she first met him, asking me all kinds of nosy questions. I think she just doesn't like the fact that I have decided to move out and this is her way of trying to keep me under her thumb. She's probably even more paranoid now that her only daughter has got herself pregnant. One junkie son and one pregnant teenage daughter. What kind of a mother is she?!

'I'm not listening to another word of this,' I turned and stalked out of the room. 'Thank you for the meal Jane, but you don't need to worry yourself any more. We won't be coming round here again!'

Tol looked surprised when I arrived in the front room announcing that we were leaving right away. Lucy, who had rushed in from the kitchen to see what the noise was all about, looked about to cry, and Martin just looked very hurt. As I marched through the hallway with Tol at my heels, I saw a face looking through the banister. I glanced up into the bewildered eyes of Simon, the new boy. I tried to give him a smile, to show that none of this was his fault. He's just a victim of the system, like me and my brother. But he didn't smile back.

Lucy followed us out into the street, buzzing around us like some irritating wasp and pleading with me not to go. She said she hadn't meant to upset me and that "real families" are always having arguments.

'Go home Luce!' I stormed at her. 'It's time you and your mum and dad realise you don't own me. I'm not your possession.'

I did feel a bit bad when Lucy burst into tears. 'I love you Hol – you're my sister!' she wailed, black mascara trailing down her cheeks. 'I didn't mean half that stuff I said earlier. I was just angry coz you were angry at me. And just coz you and Mum had some kind of row doesn't mean you and me have to fall out!'

I did feel a bit sorry for her then. We've been best friends for years and it was sad that it had to end this way. 'Go home, Luce,' I said to her, as calmly as I could manage. 'I'll text you when I feel a bit calmer.' And like a little frightened puppy with its tail between its legs, she turned round and left.

'Wooo-hooo! Heavy stuff! What are you playing at, Holly babes? Talk about madam drama queen!' Tol turned to me, his eyes sparkling with mischief. And then I felt really angry with him as well. This was all happening coz of him and he seemed to think it was some big joke. This wasn't what I needed.

'Oh **** off yourself!' I yelled at him and marched off to the bus stop.

Tol tried to talk to me on the bus journey. He wanted to know about what had gone on between me and Jane and Lucy, but I wasn't in the mood to talk. I felt like my head was bursting with everything going on inside. I didn't know what to think about first. But there was only one thing that really mattered and that was how to keep my brother safe. Maybe I should phone Donald after all. He was a good man and I'd heard how upset and angry he was that night he was taking that poor abused kid into care. I knew he'd move mountains to get the right kind of help for Ryan.

I knew that Ryan would need to be tested for HIV. I was trying to remember everything I knew about HIV and AIDS – from all those sexual health talks at school and from the leaflets you get given by social workers and doctors. I have to say, I'd never paid a huge amount of attention because at the time I wasn't planning to do anything which would put me at risk.

What I could remember though, was that HIV doesn't necessarily lead to AIDS. In the early days lots of people died from AIDS but I was pretty sure that these days it wasn't that common for people to die from it. Because if you got early treatment for HIV you might live as long as someone who didn't have it. Which was why you needed to get tested soon as poss. But how soon? That's the bit I had no idea about.

Back at St Mark's Crescent, Tol kissed me as soon as we were through the front door of the building. I meant to push him away to show him I was still incredibly mad with him but there's something about that boy...It felt really good and I'd have liked nothing more than to forget everything and go with those feelings. But I wasn't quite ready to tell him about Ryan yet, so I needed an excuse to keep Tol out of the flat. And besides, I knew my little brother would sleep better if I was in the same room with him. So I said I needed some space and Tol would have to sleep upstairs.

'OK Hol, have it your way,' Tol said sounding irritated, 'But you know where to find me if you change your mind. I'll be in that horrible little room at the top of the house, where the fan's not working. And no doubt my dear friend Stefan will listen to some deeply intellectual science programme on the World Service till way past dawn – not loud enough for me to hear the words but just loud enough to do my head in.'

Now who was the drama queen? 'Maybe later, if I feel better,' I said pressing against his warm body for a moment before pulling away. 'It's that "time of the month",' I told him casually, as I led the way upstairs. 'And I turn into a fire-breathing monster, so you'll probably be safer on your own tonight.'

'Aah,' he said, raising an eyebrow in a knowing way – which caused my heart to do a whole gym display, landing on the mat with a triple somersault into splits. 'Of course, PMT, when women are allowed to kill men without any need for an excuse. No wonder you were behaving like a crazee person earlier.'

'Exactly,' I said lying through my teeth and not particularly liking his patronising tone. But what he didn't know was that now my anger was fizzling out I was also feeling rather passionate. I was really struggling with the urge not to pull him through the front door. But I was Holly the girl who was always in control, and I wasn't going to do anything stupid now. So I kissed him once more, then pushed him firmly away and closed the door before I changed my mind.

Ryan was awake and lying on my bed watching a repeat of a really crap detective series on TV. The curtains were closed although there was still sunlight outside, and the room smelt stale and stuffy. He looked up at me and tried to manage a smile, but I could tell it was difficult. His skin felt cold, almost clammy when I put my arms around him. I rocked him gently like a baby for a few minutes and I felt his tears leaking down the side of my neck.

We watched a film on TV – something pointless and much too violent – but Ryan seemed to be kind of absorbed in it, so that was OK with me. I guess I fell asleep somewhere round midnight.

And I've been writing this diary for hours and hours, and Ryan is still asleep. Time to wake him up and make him eat something.

TUESDAY 18 AUGUST

11am

It feels a bit like Groundhog Day. Here I am again writing this diary while my kid brother sleeps. It's a scorching day outside and I'm stuck in here. And not much good stuff happened yesterday. I tried to act like normal and do some normal stuff but it wasn't easy.

I rang up about some of those jobs in the paper. Unfortunately the one I really fancied had already gone, but there's some work going in the post room at a warehouse and a clothes shop that's looking for a Saturday girl. And a local café that wants someone to do three evenings a week. None of them are really me, but I just want something that brings in some money. (My perfect holiday job would be at an art gallery. I'd show people around and maybe serve them a small glass of champagne if they looked like they were about to buy one of the most expensive pictures. Of course, those pictures would be mine, and the price tag would be £40,000 or something like that.)

At the café they were too busy to speak to me but told me to 'pop in sometime' which didn't sound promising, especially as it's the other side of the city. And at the warehouse I got to talk to a bored sounding secretary who said she'd 'send me the application form'. The phone at the clothes shop was on voicemail but I left my brightest, perkiest message, telling them how keen I was to work for them and how, as an art student, I was very passionate about fashion. I made sure I repeated my mobile number twice – very slowly. Mrs Wilson told me once that she was trying to find a part-time nanny when her kids were little. This perfect sounding person rang up and left a message. But when it got to leaving her phone number, the person just gabbled and Mrs W couldn't make it out, however hard she tried. She hoped that the person would ring again, but they never did (and they didn't have all those last number things you get these days). She always told me to keep trying – if you leave a message, then don't just wait for ever to get a reply. Phone back in a couple of days and ask whether they got your message. Not in a pushy way or anything, but just sounding efficient – and keen. People like enthusiasm; there's far too many bored-sounding people around these days, so I always make sure I sound upbeat when I make an important call.

Jane sent me a text saying *Holly please call me*. She put a kiss on it so she's trying to be nice, but I'm not going to respond to it. Nothing from Lucy which is good. And nothing from Tol either, which was a teensy bit worrying. But I'm not going to be one of those girls who chases after blokes. I'm much too sorted to behave like that. So I just sent him a really cool text saying *How's things? H xx* but it was a long time before I got any kind of answer. About midnight I got this text back saying *Babe you are like the sun and im like the caterpillar sleepin in it. Love u always.* It didn't make a lot of sense but Tol can be like that sometimes. It's probably coz he was a drama student and everyone knows how up their own bottoms they can get. Anyway it was nice that he said he loved me.

Last night was like the hottest night ever and I couldn't sleep and Ryan whimpering in his sleep was horrible to listen to. So I used the time to do some research on the old internet. There's loads of private clinics offering immediate HIV tests with instant results for £100 or more. It's not like I begrudge my little brother anything but that kind of money would make a huge dent in my savings. I need money for bills and stuff and I'm having to buy food for me and Ryan which is costing me more, and I lent Tol that £10 the other day, so it's not like I'm exactly flush with the stuff. But if that's the only way, I'll find it somehow coz he's my brother and you have to do things for your own flesh and blood.

There are these sexual health clinics run by the NHS and they don't charge – but you don't get the results as fast. And if I took Ryan in and said he was my brother, would they get suspicious that he looks so young? Maybe think he was only 11 or 12 and insist I get social services involved, which is like the last thing we need?

Also, I found out that the first test couldn't tell you everything. Even if you test clear the first time it isn't a guarantee you definitely haven't got it. You need to be tested again after three months, coz that's how long it can take for the antibodies that cause HIV to start showing up in your body.

But you still need to know if you're infected, because the sooner you get diagnosed, the sooner you can start treatment to stop you getting really ill.

Round about sevenish this morning I was looking up stuff on the Terence Higgins Trust website when I realised that Ryan was standing behind me. 'What you lookin' at?' he asked, his voice edged with suspicion.

'You startled me, little bro. How long you been there?' I said, giving myself time to think of an answer.

'Long enough,' he replied, his voice sounding flat and drained by unhappiness. 'You think I'm gonna die of AIDS, sis?'

I replied that no, of course I didn't think any such thing. 'But it might not be a bad idea to have a test,' I said, trying to sound as casual as possible. 'You don't know what diseases those men might have had...not that I'm suggesting you have it or anything, just that you need to get tested.'

'Yeah well, I don't feel like I've got the plague or nothin',' Ryan said, immediately defensive. 'There's no mega boils oozing puss on my body if that's what you're worried about.'

'What you talking about little brother? With this boils and stuff?'

'Well they say AIDS is the gay plague – like it's god's punishment for being a queer. An' we did the Black Death at school an' that was a plague. People got these black sores which went all gunky and everything.'

I didn't know whether to laugh or cry. 'AIDS isn't a plague like the black death, stupid!' I told him severely. 'And it's not a punishment for anything – just a disease that you want to avoid. If you can.'

'It's god's punishment for people who are queer. That's what my mate Tyler says.'

'And does your mate Tyler also think the world is flat? And that if you sail too far in a boat, you'll probably fall off the end?'

Ryan smiled briefly, 'Yeah, probably. He's not too bright, my mate Tyler.'

'So why are you believing this total rubbish he's telling you?'

Ryan shrugged. 'Anyway sis, if I got it I don't wanna know. What's the point? We all got to die of somethin.'

I gave Ryan several reasons why it was essential to get tested as soon as possible. Not getting worse and not risking giving it to other people in the future, being two of them; and the third being the fact that his big sis loves him and doesn't want him to suffer, when he doesn't have to. 'I'm not saying you've got it, Ryan, but if there's any risk, you have to get checked. If you haven't got it you get the good news that you're clear. And if you do have it, then you get these really good treatments that help you stay well.'

'Yeah well, maybe I don't care if I'm going to die,' Ryan said when I'd finished my explanation. And it felt like someone had just kicked me in the stomach.

'But I do,' I said, trying to act as cool as possible. 'Now go and have a shower. You stink something gross – boils or no boils.'

Now he's back in bed again, sleeping for England. Thank god Nathan was around earlier and we had a bit of a natter. He didn't ask much and I didn't tell him anything Ryan wouldn't want me to. But I know he cares about my brother coz he's a nice, sensitive bloke though he'd hate me saying that. He asked me about Lucy too, but I said that me and Lucy were no longer friends. He just said, 'Shame,' and he sounded quite sad.

Later

Strictly it's probably tomorrow but I'm not starting a new day just to say this. I tried Donald again but again I just got his voicemail. I said it was urgent and he needed to call me. There's no point trying his manager coz she's not much good. Donald's never said as much but I know he thinks that. Anyway I'm not telling important stuff to anyone except Donald. Maybe he really is in Spain or somewhere, trekking up mountains or canoeing or cycling with lots of other lonely middle-aged men who drink lots of beer in the evenings and say how glad they are they don't have wives or whatever. He didn't say he was going away but maybe it was like an impulse thing. Maybe that thing with the boy with the cigarette burns was really getting to him.

I texted Tol today and said something really casual like *Catch u later, maybe?* and he texted back saying *Sure thing. Miss u babes. Lots happenin*. I guess it's a really busy time of year for his kind of work and I know he really needs the cash. He hasn't paid me back yet for that money he borrowed at the weekend. I need to see him coz I want to talk to him about Ryan. I still haven't told him that he's here and it's getting a bit mental. What if he just turns up in the middle of the night? Though to be honest I wish he would at the moment. I kind of really miss him.

Ryan's not talking to me. I tried to mention the testing thing again in passing and he went mental. Told me to mind my own business. But he is my business and I have to think of a way to get him to a clinic.

WEDNESDAY 19 AUGUST
– Late

Something happened this morning and I don't have anyone else to tell. So sorry diary, it's got to be you that I dump all this stuff on.

I'd had it this morning with not seeing Tol. I'd had this kind of nice dream about him and I'd woken up wanting to see him really bad. Then I found that I'd missed a text from him – from the night before. It said: *Sozzy babes got back real late and need my zzzzzs. Breakfast in bed, babe? Love u.* I think it was sent about two o'clock but it was hard to tell.

And it was doing my head in not having anyone to tell about Ryan. Even if he didn't know what to do, talking to someone was better than letting it all build up inside me.

I thought Tol would probably still be asleep; it was only 7.30 and earlier than he normally went to work. I tried knocking on the door a couple of times, then ended up banging quite loudly. After a few minutes I heard the shuffle of feet.

But the figure standing in the doorway wasn't my boyfriend. The guy was shorter, stockier with closely cropped brown hair. He gazed at me suspiciously before asking 'Yes?'

I realised that I'd never set eyes on Stefan before. I know Tol said the guy seemed a bit depressed and that he preferred to keep to himself. I suddenly felt a bit guilty that here was a human being whose life was every bit as important as mine was to me, living in the same building as me, who I'd never even spent a minute thinking about. Maybe it was because I was so worried about Ryan that human life seemed extra precious this morning. But whatever it was, I decided to try and be nice to this bloke.

'Sorry,' I said, giving my best smile. 'I know it's really early. But I need to speak to Tol – like really urgently. I'm Holly by the way – from downstairs. We haven't met before...I only moved in two weeks ago.'

The guy in the doorway didn't move or smile. 'Yes,' he said. 'I have seen you sometimes.'

That felt a bit creepy, but maybe if you live in the top flat, then you can look down and see people through the gap at the centre of the stairwell. Or maybe he'd seen me out of the window.

'And Ptolemy has told me about you,' he said, which surprised me even more.

'Has he?' I said, trying to make it sound really casual. 'Look, I know he's probably not up yet but I really do need to talk to him...' I was edging my way closer to stepping over the threshold.

But Stefan didn't move. 'I do not think he is in,' he said, his face a mask of stillness.

'Well he got in really late last night – and he doesn't normally go to work this early,' I persisted.

'I think he went out,' Stefan said, frowning now. 'About five o'clock this morning,' and added as an explanation, 'I do not sleep well so I hear many noises.'

'Can we just check his room – just to make sure?' Maybe Tol had gone for one of his early morning walks, but maybe he could have crept back in, without disturbing his insomniac flatmate.

The stocky guy shrugged, 'OK. We will check.' He led the way to Tol's bedroom. He tapped softly on the door and when nobody answered he put his head around the door. 'No. He is not there,' Stefan said, closing the door behind him.

I felt quite irritated by the way this guy was behaving. This was my boyfriend's bedroom and here was his flatmate (who by all accounts he hardly ever spoke to) acting like some kind of gate-keeper. 'Yeah well, there's something I need from the room – something I need to get. That's what I wanted to talk to him about,' I insisted, determined now that if I couldn't speak to Tol at least I could be surrounded by some of his things. Like one of those soppy women in romantic novels, I suddenly had this stupid desire to lie on his bed and bury my nose in his pillows.

Stefan's eyes widened now, alive with suspicion – or was it some kind of fear?

'It's OK,' I assured him. 'I'm Tol's girlfriend. He won't mind me going into his room. I've been in before.'

And I had been in twice before, but only twice. And both times when Tol had assured me he'd 'just tidied up' (although it never looked like it to me). He'd never seemed that keen on the idea of me visiting him there. But I didn't care now. The wildest suspicions were racing through my head. Maybe some other girl was lying in his bed, fast asleep. And if Stefan was trying to protect me from this, it was very kind of him but I needed to know. I pushed past Stefan and threw open the door.

The room looked much the way it looked last time, only half lived in. Saul's stuff was piled in boxes against all of one wall, and with the desk and the cupboard, that left only room for a bed and two chairs. Tol had formed this heap round the bed of his own clothes and bits and pieces, which looked even messier than the time he said he'd tidied it. The attic roof sloped to a point high above and one large dormer window was flung wide to let in the air, but the room stank of the smell of burning.

For a silly moment I wondered if Tol was burning the notes I'd written him during the last week. Maybe on Sunday he'd decided it was all over and he'd been avoiding me coz he was getting ready to tell me and the burning was symbolic. But as I looked around for evidence of this, I saw a small piece of silver foil crumpled on the floor, with a sticky black liquid seeping out the side of it. And beside it a small tube, made from another piece of silver paper. I'd seen pictures of that on the web and I knew what it was.

I hadn't slept all night and I'd been worrying for days. Otherwise there's no way I'd have reacted like I did. I couldn't get my breath and started to panic. I've never had a panic attack before but it was well frightening. I felt like my heart was about to leap out of my body and I just couldn't get my breath, however hard I tried.

I felt hands on my shoulders, Stefan steering me out of the door and towards the kitchen, where I was pushed firmly towards a chair. 'Sit,' Stefan commanded in a voice that I wasn't going to disobey. 'Now give me your wrist.'

Meekly I obeyed, too scared now to do anything else. I was sure I was about to suffocate.

Stefan pulled up a chair beside me and taking my hand, he placed it on the kitchen table, resting two fingers on the pulse at my wrist.

'I tap the rhythm of your pulse,' he said. 'You must concentrate. Think about nothing else. Just my tapping.'

My pulse was obviously very fast from the rate his fingers were drumming but gradually the speed of the tapping slowed. I was still gasping for breath but I could feel some air getting into my lungs now, and gradually my shoulders stopped heaving. After a while the tapping got even slower and I realised I was breathing normally again.

'Hey,' I said, when I'd drunk the glass of water Stefan gave me, 'That was amazing. How did you learn to do that?'

The young man next to me shrugged. 'When the bombing happened in Sarajevo I was a little child. It was hard to be calm and sometimes I hyperventilate. My mother, she was a therapist. She taught my older sister this. And she taught me how to do it – when I was a bit older.'

'That must have been so scary,' I said, wanting to get him to talk – anything to take my mind of the fact that my boyfriend was a heroin user. 'And your mother, your sister, where are they now? I mean, what happened to them?'

But Stefan just shook his head. 'Some things I cannot talk about.'

We sat in silence for a few minutes and then Stefan said, 'You did not know? About Ptolemy?'

And I knew what he meant. I said, 'Yeah,' but like him, I couldn't really say any more.

'It is hard,' he said. 'I knew when I first met him. During the war, people had to escape the pain, the despair...somehow. They tried many things. One of the boys I came here with, his uncle died from the overdose. He had a habit himself, but he said it was only a small one. He said it did not harm him. I think you will find that Ptolemy will tell you the same.'

I guessed he probably would. I knew that some people claim to use heroin for years and never have any side effects. But I also knew that heroin screwed up many people's lives – and killed some people. It wasn't something I wanted my boyfriend involved with. And more than anything what really got to me were the lies. Tol had promised me that after the "small lie" about working at the café, there were no other secrets between us. So what else was he lying about?

Also I felt so stupid. I'd told Jane that she was wrong, I'd told Cathy she was misguided. I had honestly believed that at the time. Tol had made me look such a fool. If only I didn't love him so much

I would never want to see him again. But unfortunately I did love him. So along with my brother, I now had to save him too.

I got to my feet. 'Thank you Stefan,' I said. 'I'm sorry I got so upset. You've been really nice to me. But please don't say anything to Tol. I want to talk to him about this – but I have a lot on my mind at the moment. I need to find the right time.'

Stefan followed me to the door, frowning all the way. I wondered if he ever smiled or whether he had anything to smile about. But as I stepped onto the landing, he spoke my name. As I turned, he held out his hand and I took it, and we shook hands very solemnly. 'Take good care,' was all he said.

To my surprise, Ryan and Nathan were sitting at the breakfast table when I returned. They both looked at me really reproachfully.

'You left the milk out sis – before you went up to see lover boy,' Ryan told me, accusingly.

'It's fine, it's only been out the fridge for a little while,' I told them, sniffing at the milk quickly. It did smell a bit cheesy but I'd smelt worse. 'And I wasn't seeing Tol. I just went upstairs to get something and I met Stefan and we sort of got talking.'

'You shaggin' him as well, sis?'

I really wanted to slap my little brother but I don't believe in violence.

'You make a lot of friends,' Nathan said pointedly, ignoring Ryan's stupid comment. 'That Stefan guy never speak to me. I don't think he like black people.'

'Do you ever speak to him?' I asked, 'He's probably used to people being prejudiced against him coz he's Eastern European.'

'Eastern Europeans are takin' all the jobs,' Nathan said, gazing into his cereal bowl.

I was about to start a lecture about racism working several ways when I saw the twinkle in Nathan's eye. 'Sure,' I said. 'If I thought you really meant that, I'd pour that milk all over you...'

I glanced at Ryan to make sure he realised this was a joke. I didn't want him thinking that I was ignoring a bit of blatant racism so casually. If he thought I didn't care about racism then maybe he'd think I thought that discrimination against gay people – or bisexual people, or people who weren't sure what they were but maybe were a little bit different – was alright. My little brother had spent too long around bigots who didn't think carefully enough about what they said. It was my job to set him a good example.

But Ryan was only going through the motions of having breakfast with us. As he shovelled Coco Pops into his mouth, his mind was clearly very far away.

I don't want to write much more about today. It really wasn't a good day. After the shock about Tol, I tried to keep busy with lots of practical things. I tidied up the flat first of all, and did a load of washing. Cleaning things makes me feel in control. I did some thinking while I was whisking the vacuum cleaner around (miraculously it had survived unharmed from Mel and Keesha's party). And I set myself some deadlines. I'd spend the rest of the day trying to persuade Ryan to agree to an HIV test but if he wouldn't agree, then tomorrow I would try Donald one last time. And I'd go down and register with my new doctor's surgery and see what they could do to help me. And I would talk to Tol before the evening. I didn't want that conversation hanging over me for too long.

I texted Tol – wherever he was – and I said: *I knw about yr problem. I shld be angry that uv lied but I do luv u. We v 2 talk. Where cn I meet u?*

I wanted to be harder on him than that, but I was starting to realise how weak men are – all men. (OK, maybe there are some exceptions like Donald and Martin, and maybe that bloke Stefan seemed pretty solid.) I had thought once that Tol was different, but he wasn't. But I would save him. I knew I could.

But Ryan wouldn't talk to me. He just shook his head every time I tried to bring up the subject of HIV testing. 'It don't matter sis,' he said. And he just switched off when I tried to tell him all the reasons why it did. And Tol wasn't answering my text. I tried to call him a couple of times but each time I got his voicemail. In the message I said I was sad more than angry, but we simply had to talk.

I nearly said something about Ryan but I didn't think Tol would be that interested in my brother. To be honest, he hadn't paid much attention when I'd told him about his disappearance.

It's now midnight and I'm sitting here again, writing my diary. And I've achieved absolutely nothing. Ryan is asleep and the room is so hot I think I will melt. I'm going out to sit on the stairs for a bit coz it's the only cool place I can think of. And if Tol tries to enter or leave the building, he won't be able to avoid me.

THURSDAY the something — (I don't know what today's date is, and I'm not sure I care)

I'd like to end my day by writing about some good news, but lately there doesn't seem to be any good news around. If I was to take everything that happened today and put it through a sieve, like they do with wheat – to sort out the good stuff from the bad stuff – I wonder what I'd find.

Under good stuff, I received a card from Mrs Wilson. It had been forwarded from Jane and Martin's to my new address. Mrs Wilson was thanking me for my card and saying she really appreciated my support. It had been a terrible time, but knowing that other people cared so much about her really helped. She hoped I'd managed to arrange my move – and she wondered if I'd like to meet up with her and go to the new exhibition which was coming to the art gallery next month. She gave me her mobile number.

The other nice thing that happened today was Nathan. He's not good with words but he has this way of just being there in a really supportive way – of letting me know that he's there for me if I need him. Like he senses I'm having a bad time and he wants me to know he's on my side.

And I did have a nice snog with my boyf today, who is still sexy

– even when he's being an idiot.

Then there's going to be a list of OK stuff – things that are more positive than negative. On this list I'm putting:

Found out on the internet that NHS sexual health clinics will see a 14-year-old-boy and won't ask too many questions.

My brother is still here and hasn't run away yet

An application form arrived for the warehouse job. It goes on for ages but at least I think I have plenty of the right kind of skills. It might be a bit boring but the money is even better than they said in the advert.

Ahmina rang and left a message on my phone saying she was sorry she hadn't been in touch but her father-in-law had died very suddenly. She'd heard from Phil that I was settling in well, but I must be sure to call her if I need anything.

It clouded over today, and there were a few spots of rain. The air feels cooler and it's easier to breathe indoors.

My boyfriend is being honest with me – finally.

Before I move on to bad stuff, I'm going to include another category, to make everything a bit less bleak. It's going to be called the "Could be worse" category. In it I'm putting the following:

Lucy hasn't been in touch, which means she probably got the text I sent her, saying I was sorry our friendship had to end but it was probably better that way, and she's accepted what I've told her. I can't think about Lucy too much or I'll start to cry. I hope she doesn't hate me, I will never hate her.

Jane hasn't rung or texted since Monday. If she's mad with me I don't want to know about it at the moment.

The clothes shop rang back and asked me what experience I had. I tried to sell myself as well as I could but they said they'd had lots of applicants, several of whom had previous experience in shops. So they were only interviewing people who could prove they had "fashion retail" experience and could I provide any evidence? I asked them why they hadn't mentioned this in the job advert and the woman at the end of the line said goodbye very quickly and put down the phone. I don't think working in a dress shop would have suited me anyway. I think I'd probably try to persuade people not to buy things if I thought they were the wrong colour, or made them look too fat or too thin. Or were just too expensive. Nobody wants a shop assistant who says, 'I saw something in Oxfam or British Heart Foundation that was half the price and twice as nice.'

My brother seems to be putting on a little bit of weight – which is hardly surprising as he's still hungry all the time.

Bad things list:

I'm in love with a junkie. Tol says he's had a heroin habit for several years and he isn't planning to give it up anytime soon. Not even for me. He said he tried once before and it was too difficult. Besides, he says it isn't doing him any harm. Wish I could believe that one.

My brother is getting seriously depressed. He seemed more like his old self when he first came here but each day now he seems to be slipping back into the way he was at Kitty and Craig's.

My brother seems to be determined to believe that he's an evil person and that whatever bad things have happened to him it's because he deserves it.

My brother is starting to get quite aggressive again. He's so angry inside and he's lashing out at everyone who annoys him, even very slightly. He bites my head off almost every time I try to talk to him about anything to do with the future. Today he was really snippy with Nathan, who tried to be nice to him. Thank goodness Nathan stayed in the "being nice" category, which is why I put him on the first list.

I'm feeling really scared. And I don't really know how to cope. I hate this so much, because more than anything else in the world I really hate being out of control.

I think that's all for today. I wish now I'd started with the bad things list first and then worked my way to the good things. Maybe by tomorrow I can move some of the bad things onto the good things list.

FRIDAY 21 AUG

Today I'm going to deal with the bad things first and then end up with the good things. I hope there are going to be enough good things. It hasn't felt like a good day – but maybe I'll surprise myself.

The worst thing today was definitely Ryan. Well, not Ryan himself but the way he is. He's just getting more and more distant again. He started talking again about doing all sorts of stupid things today. It didn't help that he heard me having a row with Tol about the drugs thing. He said to me afterwards that he thought I was "over-reacting" and why was I such a goody-goody? I told him that I wasn't over-reacting and that even if Tol says he's totally in control of his habit, I didn't really believe him. Being dependent on anything isn't good for you, and besides there's always the risk of an overdose or some kind of infection (he admitted to me that he injects it sometimes although he usually inhales it). Then there's the risk of taking heroin that's been cut with soap powder or aspirin or scouring powder or ground-up plastic – and who wants that kind of stuff going into their body? Tol certainly can't afford to buy the totally pure stuff, which is how some of those doctors or really wealthy people manage to keep a habit going for years without killing themselves.

I've tried really hard to keep Tol and Ryan apart, because I just had a bad feeling about it. I think now it was because I didn't really 100 per cent trust Tol – which is an awful thing to admit. But he has lied about lots of things now and I can't totally trust him not to tell someone about my brother being here. But today Tol arrived on the doorstep about 7am – banging on the front door and demanding to be let in. He wanted me to let him into my bedroom but I said I couldn't because I had a visitor. Then he got all narky and said I was obviously sleeping with another man and if it was only a friend, why hadn't I told him if I had a girlfriend staying? And I said he was being daft and he said I was the one who was being daft, and if the person in my room was "just a friend" then why didn't I wake them up and introduce them to him? Or at least open the door a bit so he could see them sleeping? I said that was even crazier and was a rude thing to do to my visitor, but he said that if I wasn't prepared to do this then I was definitely hiding something.

I said he had no right to talk about people hiding things, when he'd lied about something as major as being a junkie. And that's when he tried to tell me that I didn't know what I was talking about, that it wasn't like he was going to die of it or anything.

Thank goodness Nathan is a really sound sleeper. You could let off bombs and he would sleep through it. I wouldn't have blamed him at all for being furious about Tol waking him up at this time of the morning.

But the noise did wake someone. I was just telling Tol that he had no right to doubt me when he lied so much himself, when I realised that Ryan was standing in the doorway, watching us row.

'Who the hell are you?' Tol spun round to confront my little brother, but I could hear from his voice that he was more surprised than angry. With his slight build and pixyish face, Ryan definitely doesn't look old enough to be some kind of secret lover.

'Who the hell do you think he is?' I demanded of Tol, feeling fiercely protective of my little bro.

So that's how Tol and Ryan met and it wasn't at all the way I'd planned it. Tol couldn't understand why I hadn't told him before that Ryan was here – and I snapped back that was because he didn't seem to be particularly concerned about anything that concerned me. And Tol said this was a total lie, and that he loved me and that maybe he kept things from me because he didn't want to hurt me, but he just couldn't understand why I hadn't told him the incredible news that Ryan was safe.

What could I say to that? With Ryan standing there in front of us? I couldn't think of any explanation that wouldn't give away how worried I was about my brother's health. 'Ryan didn't want me to tell anyone,' was all I could mumble.

'Are you seriously telling me that Nathan doesn't know he's here?' Then Tol deliberately turned his back on me and approached Ryan, holding out his hand. 'Sorry mate, didn't mean to talk about you like you're invisible or something. I'm Ptolemy by the way – but everyone calls me Tol. I'm your sister's boyfriend. Though you probably wouldn't believe it from what you just heard.'

I wondered how Ryan would react. Tol is pretty charming when you first meet him but Ryan was super wary at the moment. But to my surprise, Ryan took the outstretched hand for a moment and shook it, and there was this moment of manly bonding. 'My sister is like that,' Ryan said. 'She don't trust nobody.'

I could have throttled my little brother! All that trouble I'd gone to so I could keep him being here secret, and that's how he repays me!

I stormed past both of them, slamming the bedroom door closed behind me. I scrambled out of my pyjamas and pulled on a pair of jeans and a t-shirt. It was still looking pretty overcast and would probably rain at any moment. But I didn't care. I'd been cooped up indoors for too long. I needed to get out and clear my head.

Tol tried to stop me leaving. 'Calm down Hol,' he said, 'your brother and I are getting on fine. He's telling me about the music he likes – some of it's a bit radical even for me, but hey, we've found something in common. I wish you'd told me before; I can help you keep him occupied while he's here.'

'I need to be alone,' I said, pushing him aside, but he followed me to the doorstep. He caught me around the waist and pulled me around to face him. He lifted my chin and kissed me, very passionately. My common sense told me to pull away but every other bit of me wanted him so badly. 'I have to go,' I said eventually, wriggling out of his embrace, but already planning how I could manage to spend some time alone with him later on. (I make myself really mad sometimes. How can you love someone so much and be so angry with them at the same time?)

It was pouring by the time I got outside, but I didn't care. It helped me to think. There were a few people about, going to work or taking their children to childminders, but overall the streets were quiet. It's been so dead in this city in August, everybody just seemed to give up. But the people I did see today looked refreshed and, if this doesn't sound too weird, a bit grateful. Maybe as though they were thirsty plants and the rain was quenching them. I wished the rain could wash away all my problems so easily.

I'd brought the mobile with me and I knew I had to find Donald. It was the reason I'd left the flat, wasn't it? Otherwise I wouldn't be walking out leaving my brother with Tol, who is hardly the sort of role model my little brother needs right now.

Donald told me once that he's normally at his desk by 8am, so I was going to try him on his landline. If he was around and there was something wrong with his mobile, it could be the best place to catch him.

It was nearly eight by the time I found somewhere to call from. I went into a small park where there were some old trees, with seats under them. The leaves on the trees were so big and their growth was so dense that they formed their own giant umbrella, and the rain couldn't get through. I dialled Donald's number but it was engaged which seemed like a good sign. I didn't really want to leave a message. I decided to give it a few more minutes before I called back.

While I waited I flicked through my contact lists. There were some people I didn't need in my life and it was time I got rid of them. I was going to delete Lucy and Jane's numbers permanently. Usually when I make up my mind about something I stick to it, because someone once told me it was weak to change your mind. I'm not so sure about that any more, I've noticed that a lot of celebrities and politicians change their minds – and nobody thinks they're weak for doing that. But last week I was so sure that Tol was my soulmate; I was convinced he was the only man I would ever want to be with. Today I don't know any more. Today I wish there was some button I could press, so I could stop having feelings for him. But maybe that's coz I have to learn to work things out with him. Maybe once we get through the current problems our lives will be better. Especially when I can get him to kick his heroin habit.

But I didn't delete Jane's number or Lucy's. I realised that I knew the house number off by heart from all those years of answering the phone when Jane or Martin weren't around and I was the only adult there. So I just contented myself with deleting Ahmina's number. I know she thought she did an OK job but she hadn't exactly been the perfect social worker. Although I guess it wasn't her fault that her father-in-law chose to die just at the point when I moved into my own place. And it wasn't like I really needed her. It's just that it's her job to be there for me. I was getting pretty sick of people who let me down.

I tried Donald again but the number was still engaged. And the rain was falling even harder. I was getting shivery and wished I'd brought a jacket. It wouldn't help Ryan if I got a really bad cold or flu or something, and couldn't look after him. So I left a quick message for Donald: *I've heard from Ryan – but it's difficult. He's scared – and it seems like some really bad stuff has happened to him. I can't pressure him...I don't know what to do, but I'm dead worried about him. Please call me back, soon as poss.*

It wasn't exactly the truth but I was worried that if Donald knew Ryan was with me he might feel he had to call someone and get them to check out the flat. Why was everything so complicated? When was I going to be able to have some time for me, just to enjoy the summer and get ready to be an art student? I'd been dreaming of this time for so long and now other people were seriously screwing it up.

I walked back to St Mark's Crescent, trying Donald's phone again a couple of times, but he was still not answering. Who was he talking to so early in the morning?

When I got back, Tol was gone and Ryan was in bed, eating a bowl of Rice Krispies with at least three inches of sugar on the top. He told me with a scowl that the supply of Coco Pops had run out.

I asked Ryan what he thought of Tol and he said he was a 'pretty cool guy'. I was still annoyed with Ryan for his comment earlier that I didn't trust anybody, but I wasn't in the mood for a row. However, it seemed that Ryan was. He started asking why I'd made such a big thing of my boyfriend using a little "gear". I told him that it was a complex issue and wasn't something I really felt in the mood to talk about. Ryan then started saying that I obviously didn't know what I was on about. That "everyone" knew that there was an international conspiracy to make people think drugs were harmful because that kept them expensive, so people got rich from selling them illegally. I said that he was oversimplifying things a bit. OK, some drugs maybe weren't as harmful as people thought, but in my opinion heroin definitely wasn't something to mess with. In my foster homes I'd spent time around kids whose parents had ruined their own lives, and their children's lives, with a serious drug problem. I wasn't saying that heroin was the only culprit, but I'd seen too much bad stuff to have any doubts about the damage it could do.

Ryan asked why I continued to hang out with Tol if I didn't like his habit. I said that was because I hoped I'd be able to help him get the right support to come off it. Ryan seemed to think this was incredibly funny and said again that I had 'no idea'.

'You seem to be a bit of an expert on this subject, little bro,' I said, trying not to show I was getting ruffled.

'Yeah well, I bin on the street – which you haven't.' Which was the sort of answer I'd secretly been dreading.

'Are you telling me you've tried it?' I asked, watching very carefully how he would respond, knowing all the time that was a stupid question to ask a teenage boy. Challenge them about anything and they'll almost always lie rather than lose face.

'Maybe,' Ryan told me with a smug grin on his face.

I was quite pleased with the way I kept my cool, when really I wanted to slam the door and lock my brother in the room, and scream at him for being such a stupid little idiot. 'OK,' I said, 'Then you probably know it's usually a very nice experience the first time. But few people who do it once can ever stop there. And with all your knowledge, you'll also know that you need a bit more each time. And that the average heroin user spends about £100 a day on their habit. You'll also know that a really big danger lies in all the crap they mix with it coz very few people can afford the pure stuff.'

(I do my homework. I've spent hours looking on the web. I

could appear on Mastermind answering questions on the origin of the phrase "chasing the dragon" and tell you what percentage of people thought that inhaling heroin was safer that injecting it, and how many thought it was just as risky because this method was more likely to cause brain damage.)

'I need a coffee,' I told Ryan, but really I wanted an excuse to go and check my mobile and see if Donald had replied yet. (I'd turned the volume off and kept it in my pocket. I didn't want to risk Ryan getting suspicious.)

'Coffee is a drug,' Ryan told me, getting even smugger.

'Yes – so is anything that has caffeine in it. You're probably a bit addicted to Coco Pops and I'm probably just as addicted to coffee. And chocolate. But as far as I'm aware neither of them are Class A drugs because they're not massively dangerous. I'm not claiming that it's healthy to drink as much coffee as I do...'

'They're still drugs.'

'Grow up!' I snapped at Ryan, and stormed out to the kitchen. His skewed logic was starting to irritate me – and worry me as well. It was definitely time to get help from someone.

But Donald's phone still seemed to be going straight to voicemail. Maybe he was taking some time off and he'd switched his mobile off for the day. Typical social worker, I thought, never available when you need them.

I really wished I had someone to talk to but there was no one I could think of. Maybe I shouldn't have deleted Ahmina's number earlier, but what good would she be in this kind of situation? She'd probably fuss a lot and make things worse. If I was still speaking to Jane I'd be tempted to call her, but I wasn't ready for that. OK, she was a little bit right about Tol, but that didn't give her the right to interfere in my business.

We needed milk and cereal and other stuff, so I escaped outside. It was dry now and the sun was beginning to come out from behind the clouds. Seeing the sun again made me feel a bit better. Funny how you can get sick of something, then miss it really badly after it's not around for a few hours.

In the end I decided to call Tol. To tell him what I was worried about. He picked up after three rings sounding very bored. 'What you doing?' I asked.

'Sitting in a café and watching some men carrying frozen meat from one van to another van. One van is white and the other van is white but has a blue band round the bottom. I can definitely recommend a career as a private eye to anyone wanting to broaden their horizons. Especially if they're excited by the idea of an illegal trade in pig carcasses.'

I said that it sounded exciting and was clearly even better than in the films. I then asked him if he was able to speak for a few minutes, and he said he was.

I told him that I was worried about Ryan and needed his help. I didn't go into detail but I told him that Ryan was pretty vulnerable at the moment. I said that I needed to keep Ryan as safe as possible and that whatever he, Ptolemy, did as an adult was his own business – even if I didn't approve of it. But that I certainly didn't want my little brother mixed up, under any circumstances.

'Babe!' Tol exclaimed, sounding really hurt. 'I'm not some drug pusher you know, going round trying to get little kiddies hooked!'

I assured him that I didn't think he was. But I told him that Ryan had overheard our conversation earlier – and that I had reason to believe Ryan had already been experimenting. 'So I really need you on my side with this one, Tol. I don't want my brother thinking this is something cool that he should try. So if he asks you about it...'

'I'll say that it's not something I would recommend to anyone else. Because nobody really chooses to be a smackhead if they're honest – it's far too expensive for a start...'

Tol's response filled me with a sense of relief. Not only was he going to support me with my brother, but this was so much better than the attitude he'd given me when we discussed this before. 'I love you Tol,' I told him, and I meant it.

I hoped Ryan would be safe while I was out. Anyway it was probably good to show him that I trusted him not to run away. If he thought I was watching his every move, he'd be bound to try and escape.

I bought fruit and salad things from the market. I didn't feel in the mood to cook so I got ready-made quiches for supper. Goodness knows how much money I've spent on food this week. But I don't want Nathan to feel he is paying to feed an army of visitors. Thank goodness there was this two for one offer, so I was able to get plenty to go round. Not that Tol ever eats much. He's tried to tell me that he'd never had much of an appetite, even before the heroin, but I think he's just forgotten how good food can taste.

When I was leaving the supermarket, somebody called my name. It was Gina, one of the girls from my class. She'd been kind to me when I first started and we'd hung out a bit over the years, and I suppose you could call her a friend. She said she was glad she'd bumped into me and we gave each other our phone numbers. Which is probably one of the things I'm going to put on my list of "good things that happened today". I'd kind of forgotten how much I like Gina. I promised that I'd call her really soon, and I think I meant it.

So Gina is going on my list of good things for today. Along with me and Ryan not having any more rows today coz he spent the evening watching football and DVDs with Nathan. Which gave me and Tol a bit of time to ourselves, which was dead nice. But he had to go about eleven coz he had work in the morning and anyway I had my little brother to think about.

SATURDAY 22 AUGUST

Today went pear-shaped – again. This morning was OK. Nathan and me managed to drag Ryan down to the park for a bit. It was a fab day and it would've been criminal to spend it all indoors. We were just messing around coz we're all too old really to play footie in the park, and the boys were telling me I was no good, which was definitely a lie. But Ryan did laugh a bit – even if it was just at his poor sister.

We had a bit of a picnic with some crisps and sandwiches and stuff, but then Ryan said the sun was bringing on one of his headaches and we had to go back to the house. He slept like all afternoon, so I did some more reading for my course.

There was another call from Kitty today but I ignored it. She's been trying to call me all week but I've been avoiding her. I just don't know what to say to her. I hate lying, so it's best not to speak. Anyways, not till I've got hold of Donald.

At supper Ryan seemed obsessed with getting Tol's approval. He didn't want to talk to Nathan any more and it seemed my brother had no time for me either. He started telling Tol about some of the stuff his friends used to do, like stealing cars and mobiles. I wasn't sure if this was true or just something he'd heard other kids talking about. You can never be quite sure with Ryan coz he has quite a vivid imagination. But hearing this, I realised what the purse theft had been all about: Ryan trying to prove he was as tough as the other kids. Funny really, coz Tol's hardly a tough guy and he's the last person to worry about someone mistaking him for being gay. But Ryan seemed to be under the impression that Tol's drug habit made him streetwise – in every sense.

Tol was clearly lapping up the adulation from a 14-year-old kid, or maybe he just thought this was a good way to get along with my younger brother. Either way, he didn't exactly go out of his way to show Ryan that he was being a prat.

So I was really relieved when Tol finally changed the subject and started talking about his photography. To my surprise, Ryan seemed quite interested in that too and started asking some questions. And of course the conversation moved on to Tol's weird job.

Nathan and I went through to watch some TV and left them chatting in the kitchen. 'Yo bruvver OK?' Nathan asked me in a low voice as we settled on the sofa.

I shook my head and replied in an equally low tone. 'Nope. I'm really worried about him. And I've been trying to get hold of his social worker all week...'

Nathan nodded sagely. 'Probably best.'

'I need to keep an eye on him, till I hear back from Donald, his worker. He's a good bloke, he really cares about the kids he works with, well all kids actually. As I said, he's a good bloke.'

'Sure. You want that I keep an eye on him too?'

I said that would be great.

After a while Tol and Ryan came through to join us. Tol wanted to cuddle up with me and I was happy enough to be close to him. After a little while he whispered into my ear and we slipped away to my room for a bit. Ryan had settled in front of a really gory horror film and Nathan seemed to be enjoying it as well, so I thought that was safe enough. Nathan had offered to help me watch Ryan after all.

When Tol and I returned to the living room Keesha and Mel had joined the party. And party was the right word. They'd brought a bottle of vodka and a bottle of Southern Comfort with them and seemed to be tucking in. Nathan turned a worried face to me, mouthing something, but I could guess already. Keesha was sitting next to my little brother pouring out a very small portion of alcohol into a tiny glass. 'This your lot likkle boy,' she said, handing him the glass. 'You much too young to have this, anyhows.'

'So you're plugging my little brother with spirits, now?' I hoped my voice sounded light – quite jokey. I didn't want a scene with Keesha.

'Hey the love birds return!' Keesha grinned at me. 'Lighten up girl. I only give your brother the very teeniest, weeniest taste of this stuff. It ain't for wasting on likkle boys.'

Tol flopped down on the couch next to Nathan and Mel, who was sitting opposite, shot him a look that would have killed a weaker man. Tol reached immediately for a bottle and poured himself a shot. He held the bottle out to me. I wanted to say no coz I'm never that keen on neat vodka (it gives me evil headaches), but I knew this would be another sign of me being pathetic in my brother's eyes. Which was stupid of course – when have I ever cared what other people think? And wasn't it crazy to be drinking just to prove to a 14-year-old boy that I'm not as uptight as he thinks I am? But I still poured a small shot and sipped it slowly through my teeth. While thinking about how to get my bro out of this situation.

As everyone laughed and chatted, and nobody seemed to be getting too drunk or, more importantly, about to offer my brother any more alcohol, I started to relax. Nathan even went to the kitchen and got some cans of Coke, and put one in front of Ryan and myself, before opening his own. He's very thoughtful that boy. (Pity about me and Lucy. Nathan would have made a decent boyf.)

About 10.30, Keesha announced that she simply had to go out dancing and who wanted to go. Ryan looked eager but was quickly squashed by Keesha shaking her fingers at him. 'No, no, no – dis club is no place for baby-faced likkle boys like you!'

Tol glanced questioningly at me and I shook my head firmly. We would have plenty of time for going out once my brother was sorted out.

But Keesha decided to be insistent. 'C'mon girl! We can have a girls' night – you, me and Mel. Da boys can look after your brother. He won't come to no harm.'

'Yeah sis, you go. I won't come to no trouble here,' Ryan insisted, eyes wide with sincerity. But I wasn't fooled.

'I can stay Hollyberry, and keep an eye on him,' Tol volunteered. 'You should go out. You could do with some fun.'

'An' I'll be here,' Nathan assured me solemnly.

'No – thanks guys but honestly, I'm not in the mood at the moment,' I told everyone.

Keesh shrugged: 'Please yourself girl – but if you changes your mind before eleven then we'll still be here.'

Mel winked at me. 'Probably midnight – the time Keesh takes to do her hair.'

After they left, Ryan insisted on watching a DVD that Nathan had mentioned earlier. Something about zombies and surgical instruments. It didn't sound like anything I really wanted to see. But with the three boys settled comfortably on the sofa, everyone drinking coke or coffee now, I thought it couldn't harm to have some time to myself. Which is why I'm here writing this diary.

MONDAY 24 AUGUST

Jane brought my diary into the hospital. She said I needed something to stop me fretting. And she said writing it all down might help me make sense of things. Anyway, I want to have a complete record so when I look back in ten years' time and think, 'Why did that happen?' I can give myself some answers. Who knows where I'll be in ten years' time? Hopefully I'll be an artist and one day I'll find this diary of the summer I made so many mistakes, and it maybe will inspire me to paint something amazing. Of course, by then my life will be really sorted. I might have a partner who is really special, and I'll show this to him and let him read what happened.

I think I must have fallen asleep on the bed after I finished writing the diary on Saturday night. I remember Tol waking me up as he lay down on the bed beside me. I asked him where my brother was and he said my brother was fine, now watching yet another slasher film with Nathan. I said I ought to go and make him come to bed but Tol said there was no point. The boy was wide awake – he'd been doing nothing all day but cat-napping and watching TV, and I was the one that really needed the sleep. When

Tol made it clear that he intended to stay with me for a while,
I didn't need a lot of persuading.

I also remember waking up – a bit freaked out. Tol was gone
from the bed and there was no sign of my brother. I remember
dragging myself into some pyjamas and cursing under my breath
as I hurried to the living room, half expecting to find my brother
still glued to some hideous bloodfest on screen.

The TV was still on but the DVD had ended long ago and there
was just a play card repeating endlessly without any sound. At first
glance, from the doorway the room looked empty. Then I realised
that Tol was lying on the sofa, stretched out. There was a cigarette
pack on the table and an overflowing ashtray and both the bottles
from earlier were completely empty. There was lots of general
mess, screwed up sweet wrappers and all kinds of stuff lying
around. But then I looked again and the sweet wrappers weren't
sweet wrappers but pieces of tinfoil. And that smell from before
was in the air.

'What the…?' I hissed, stepping into the room to shake my
stupid boyfriend awake, and tell him to get out of my flat. And stay
out.

But I tripped over something on the floor – my brother's foot.
'You stupid…' but I never got any further. Because that's when I
saw the puke streaked all over my brother's clothes, and in his hair.
And his face looked so white that in that moment I knew he must
be dead.

I screamed so loudly I must have woken everyone in the
building. Even Tol stirred on the sofa with a dreamy, distant look
on his face. 'Chill, Hol. It's OK,' was what he said.

I can't remember all the names I called him as I told him that
it most definitely wasn't OK. But I do remember the look on his
face when he realised something serious had happened. I also
remember when he left the room, insisting he was going to call

an ambulance. And listening to the front door slam behind him as he left and knowing without a doubt that this selfish, shallow boy – who I'd loved so much – was running away.

In the panic of that moment I couldn't remember where I'd left my phone. I banged on Nathan's door but nothing wakes Nathan – especially when he's had vodka before bedtime. I was screaming and crying and rushing from room to room like a madwoman. Then I remembered someone who would be awake at this hour and tore upstairs to bang on his door.

Stefan was very calm. I couldn't find the words to explain what was happening, so he told me to show him what the matter was. With his mobile in hand he followed me downstairs and the minute he saw my unconscious brother he dialled 999. I remember the relief when I heard him say, 'Yes, it is very serious but the boy is still breathing.' He gave our address and all the details to the person at the end of the line, stopping every now and then to ask me a question. What was it that I thought he'd taken? Heroin, vodka...that was all I could think of. 'Was the heroin injected or inhaled?' he asked. Inhaled I thought, but I couldn't be sure.

Nathan was awake by the time the ambulance arrived. He came with me to the hospital and held my hand in his big, kind sweaty one.

I don't want to write much more about that night or how long we waited until the doctors confirmed that the special injection they gave him had taken effect. Or how long it was before we knew that there was no brain damage. I only vaguely remember when the policewoman I asked to see arrived, and telling her everything I could about Ptolemy, including giving her his phone number.

(Nathan and Keesha came to visit earlier and they told me they'd been talking to Stefan. Apparently Ptolemy tried to get back into the top flat – probably to pick up his stuff – but as soon as he saw the look of rage on Stefan's face he knew he was in for trouble.

Stefan had chased him out the building and down the street, but finally lost him when Ptolemy jumped over a fence. 'Stefan says he needs to get more fit,' Nathan told me. 'He's comin' to the gym wiv me tomorrow.')

I remember the joy of waking up from a doze in the waiting room, to find Jane and Lucy crouching beside me. They both held me for a very long time and I hugged them so tight I'm surprised I didn't break their ribs. I tried to say sorry and ask if they could ever forgive me but Jane said it was OK, all families have arguments sometimes and pick up the pieces – and were often closer for it. I told Jane and Lucy everything that had happened, including the details Ryan had told me about the paedophile gang and the reasons he was running away. Jane asked if I'd told the staff this and I said I had – because I didn't want anyone to be put at risk. I didn't know if nurses and doctors could be infected by treating someone who might have HIV, so I wasn't taking any more risks. I'd made enough mistakes to last a lifetime.

Jane told me that everyone makes mistakes and as things went, I'd probably coped pretty well. I had been trying to do the right things for my brother and she doubted if many young people in my situation could have handled it better. I told her she was wrong and that anyone with any sense would have stayed away from a loser like Tol. They'd have listened to the warnings when so many sensible people were trying to tell them something.

Jane says I have to stop writing in a minute. She says I need some sleep and she's taking me back to their house – just for tonight. She says that Martin really wants to see me, to check for himself that I'm OK. And that Simon has made a card for me and wants to give it to me himself. Lucy says I can borrow Mr Giraffe if I want, and I think I might take her up on the offer.

TUESDAY 25 AUGUST

I don't have much time coz we're going to the hospital soon: me and Martin and Lucy. (Jane is taking Simon to the zoo coz she's worried about him having so many nightmares and knows he's got this fixation with penguins, so she hopes they'll cheer him up.)

The police rang earlier and told me they'd checked the flats and dusted for fingerprints. They'd tried Ptolemy's phone and they tried all the numbers they found in his address book, including his parents. But Ptolemy seems to have vanished off the face of the earth. To give them credit, the police seem to be trying quite hard. Giving Class A drugs to a minor is a pretty serious offence, especially when it nearly leads to manslaughter. I hope they find him. I won't hesitate to give evidence against him.

Jane told me that Donald is coming down on Thursday. She's been talking to him a lot on the phone. He's been in hospital himself. Someone jumped the lights at a junction and hit his car, Jane said. The poor man is now on crutches, but he's coming on the train with Kitty.

WEDNESDAY 26 AUGUST

Today, me and Lucy had girl time. Jane said I needed a break from hospital and of course, it's Lucy's 16th birthday – which as usual everyone nearly forgot coz there was so much else going on. But luckily this time Jane had put it on the calendar and last night we all decorated the house while she was asleep and made her a special breakfast, and gave her lots of presents and cards and things.

So, me and Lucy went swimming and we had a pizza afterwards (which Martin paid for). We had a lot of talking to do – about the baby and all that. It was nice hanging out with Luce again.

Ryan managed a smile when I visited him this evening. He doesn't want to talk much and the doctors say he 'needs time'. Nathan came to the hospital to meet us and me, Lucy and Nathan went to a movie. I think I fell asleep coz when I woke up Nathan was holding Lucy's hand. Sweet!!

THURSDAY 27 AUGUST

Donald looks pretty battered, poor thing. He'd had to be cut out of his car. He'd been kept in the hospital for almost a week (he was pretty mad about that and said that the doctors had 'no idea about what's important'.) His manager had taken over his caseload – but she'd only been dealing with the "urgent" stuff. ('That woman has no idea either,' Donald let on, clearly too irritated to be discreet about his manager.) Kitty had volunteered to let me know– but I'd been avoiding her calls and messages so I didn't know what was happening.

Donald was kinder to me than he should have been and said it wasn't my fault. I found it hard to believe him. I was really surprised that he said he wanted me to be included in the meetings with Jane, Martin, Kitty and the hospital social worker (and Ahmina who turned up late as ever, but brought me this really cool silk scarf thing that she said might look nice in my new room, so I kind of forgave her). And to be honest, I didn't have a lot to say, because I felt I'd given up the right to be included in my brother's future. I'd let him down so badly that I was ready to hand all the decisions over to other people. But Donald said I was an "important part" of any planning for Ryan's future. He was going to need a huge amount of support to recover from the experiences he'd been through. Donald seemed far more worried that Ryan had been abused by paedophiles than that I'd nearly killed my little brother through an overdose of alcohol and heroin. One, he said, was a horrible experience that would have very long-term effects but the overdose had done no lasting harm and might eventually do some good – like making Ryan more sensible about what he took in the future.

I told the meeting that I thought Ryan was probably trying to kill himself. That he'd been talking about wanting to die and he'd probably deliberately encouraged that loser Ptolemy to let him try smoking heroin. But the hospital social worker said the psychiatrist had told him that was unlikely. The boy was clearly depressed but like lots of kids he was "sensation-hungry" and was looking for a bit of excitement to make himself feel better. The overdose probably wasn't intentional, just something that happened by accident. But they wanted to keep him in for a while, just to observe him and work out which medication might help – if any.

The plan is that as soon as Ryan is released from hospital he will move into Jane and Martin's. He will have a lot of help from the Child and Adolescent Mental Health Team as well as them. The support will help him to cope with everything he's been through – the bullying at school, his own mixed-up feelings about his sexuality – and also the deep down problems that Donald believes Ryan has always had – which is wanting some unconditional love from a father figure in his life. Something that neither Ryan's own dad, my dad or Craig had managed to get right. And we all think that Martin will be the best person to give him some of this. Martin is more than able to put up with Ryan's nonsense and he loves all the children that come to us without any conditions, however screwed up, violent or withdrawn they may be. Jane tells me that finally Simon has opened up to Martin and has told him things that he couldn't disclose to anyone else. Martin and Jane have now decided to keep Simon for as long as his local authority wants him to stay. They've decided they're not going to have any more short-term kids. Just Simon and Ryan for the moment.

'Besides, Ryan is like family already – Dad loves you like a daughter so he's going to be a bit of a second dad to your brother,' Lucy said to me, when she was finally included in the planning. Poor Lucy, as ever she's always the last person to know what's going on. But she didn't have any problems at all with the plans that had been discussed. She would move out and move in with me, in the middle flat. Nathan – who's been a total saint through this whole thing – will move upstairs for the time being to live with Stefan. (I think it's now been made official that Saul has moved in with his boyfriend.) It's a bit unusual, but everyone says it's OK for the moment, especially Phil and Cathy who have been a bit shaken up by everything and keep ringing me to ask questions about what they could have done better (maybe one day I will give them a list). Even Donald's local authority have agreed that they will pay for Lucy to move out, so that Ryan can move in. (Lucy is after all a pregnant teenager and although she's not strictly homeless, she gave up most of her childhood to fostering, so in my opinion it's time the system gave her something back.)

Lucy and I will probably row like mad about things like whose turn it is to clean the toilet, but it will be fab to have her around again. I have really missed her. I don't know yet if Lucy will keep the baby. She says she really loves the idea of a cute baby to hold and cuddle, and dress and play with. But she also loves the idea of travelling round the world and having a lot of freedom and time to just enjoy herself. She's told Nathan about the baby, but he says he's cool with that. He wouldn't mind sticking with her whatever she decides. I've never seen a guy so adoring before in my whole life. You'd think he was the cat that got the goldfish. He smiles all day long.

I've forgotten to mention about Kitty and Craig. Kitty told me Craig was devastated to hear that some stupid comment he'd made had caused so many problems. 'He thinks the world of Ryan, pet,' she told me earnestly. 'But men sometimes say daft things – well so do women I s'poose – and he needs to think harder about what he says in front of kids in the future. He's lucky that our Donald is such a sensible man, otherwise he might have said something to Lewis's social worker – and he could have been took off us, pet.'

I told Kitty that I didn't think any social worker in their right mind would take Lewis away from them, because they'd clearly done wonders with him. I told Kitty that I thought they'd both tried really hard with Ryan but it wasn't their fault that he'd always wanted to be closer to me. Kitty said I was kind to say that and she hoped I was right. I said that if it wasn't true then Ryan wouldn't have asked to see her, or asked if both of us could still sometimes visit them in Newcastle. I'm quite glad about that. I've got fond of Kitty and it will be good to go and stay with her sometimes. Anyway, I think someone will always need to be interested in Lewis's fish, and I'm quite good at doing that.

FRIDAY 28 AUGUST

I woke up in my own bedroom this morning and it felt good. I've bagged up all the little reminders of Ptolemy and put them in the bin, and it feels like my territory again. Maybe when I stop feeling so angry with Ptolemy it will start to hurt a little, but for now I'm happy to stay feeling mad.

But it felt good not to have to worry about anyone, and to know that my little bro is getting the help he needs. It seems that finally people are starting to listen to him. It was good they asked his permission before they gave him the HIV test. (It was negative but it's still early days. He'll have to have another one in three months' time.) I'm glad they listened when Ryan said that he doesn't want to see his own dad – or his aunt at the mo, because his birth dad scares him a bit, and would definitely beat him up if he knew about the "gay thing". Or get the aunt to do it for him. Donald says that because Ryan is 14, the court should respect his wishes and even if Ryan's relatives take a case to court, his relatives probably wouldn't get the right to visit him if he wasn't willing to see them. But with all these things they'll keep it open – so if Ryan feels differently he can see them again in the future.

More than anything Ryan says he wants to go and visit our mum. Not straight away and not till he feels a lot stronger. Nobody said it would be a bad idea and nobody tried to put him off. Although everyone knows it won't be easy. Jane has said she will come with us when we go because, as painful as it is, I'm not having Ryan going to visit Mum on his own.

I think that's all the loose ends gathered up now. I think my story is complete and when I read this in my artist's studio in the future I'll be able to see that although things have been difficult, some good has come out of it.

Of course if this was a fairytale, my mum would instantly get better and my dad would ring from America and send the money for us to go and visit. Real life isn't like that. But I suppose I could include one good thing which might give this story a more traditional happy ending.

Sean came to the hospital on that second day. I hardly recognised him at first. In the couple of weeks since I'd last seen him, he'd changed quite a bit. He'd had his hair cut shorter and spikier and he's started to gel it. It really suits him. He's been writing songs again and he said he was thinking of maybe joining a band when he gets to uni, so he needed to do something about his image.

I wasn't sure if it was just gratitude at first or the relief of having someone familiar around, but it felt good to have him with me. He's started ringing me and texting me again and he's even spent some time keeping my brother amused during visiting hours. I'm not really into playing computer games and I get bored after a while.

Today I found myself watching Sean a lot of the time. Watching the way his fingers are so long and graceful when he's using the keyboard, watching the way a bit of his newly cut hair flops slightly over his right eye and what a good effect this is. And realising for the first time just how good his legs look in tight jeans.

I think he sensed something was different. He asked me afterwards in the hospital coffee shop if I was "seeing anyone". I told him I had been, that the relationship had been pretty serious but was totally over now. I asked him then if he was seeing anyone and he said, 'sort of,' but then said it'd only lasted three days. 'She wasn't enough like you Holly,' he said, 'It was rather boring. She never yelled at me or bit my head off.'

'But I don't know that I did that when we were first together – she might turn out to be more like me if you give her a chance,' I told him, wondering where this conversation was going.

'Oh, you were always difficult, you were difficult right from the start,' Sean assured me. 'You've always made up your mind about something, and nothing and nobody could change it.'

'I'm sorry,' I said. 'I must have made an awful girlfriend.'

'Actually I loved it. I'd have you back tomorrow Hol – if I thought you'd be interested.'

'I am interested,' I heard myself saying, feeling a tingling sense of excitement in my stomach.

'Really?' Sean looked doubtful. 'I mean we could take it really slowly, not rush anything, just spend a bit of time together and...'

'Or we could be totally impulsive and book that trip to Paris we've always talked about...P'raps some time in the next couple of weeks, before term starts...I got some grant money through and I could pay for both of us.'

Sean clutched his forehead, mockingly dramatic. 'Somebody call a doctor! I think I'm going to faint. I mean you – doing something which hasn't been in your plans for the last two years? Holly Richards, are you feeling quite well?'

'Very well,' I said, leaning across the table to kiss his mouth. And when I next came up for air, I added, 'I have changed a bit, you know.'

BAAF books – for social workers

....

Ten Top Tips on Preparing Care Leavers
Henrietta Bond

How do young people who have grown up in care survive
without a safety net to fall back on?
How do they get through the turmoil of the late teens
and early twenties without the emotional and financial
support of a loving family behind them? In other words,
how do they make it?

This book is for all those who work with young people
who are preparing to leave care and step into life as
independent young adults, such as – social workers,
leaving care workers, residential care workers and others.
Based on the views and experiences of young people
themselves, it offers child-centred advice on: setting out
to be a great corporate parent; having high aspirations
for young people; helping care leavers achieve practical
and budgeting skills for adult life; accessing housing
and benefits; and supporting young people to live by
themselves.

Illustrated with quotations from care leavers and workers,
this book delivers a strong message – believe in and
expect the best for every young person you work with and
support them to achieve it – and tells you how to make
this a reality.

£7.95
114 PAGES
ISBN 978 1 905664 30 6

Order online at www.baaf.org.uk or by phoning BAAF
Publications on 020 7421 2604
or emailing pubs.sales@baaf.org.uk